Life
Belts

Life
Belts

Jane
Hosie-Bounar

Delacorte Press

Published by
Delacorte Press
Bantam Doubleday Dell Publishing Group, Inc.
1540 Broadway
New York, New York 10036

Library of Congress Cataloging in Publication Data

Hosie-Bounar, Jane.
    Life belts / by Jane Hosie-Bounar.
        p.   cm.
    Summary: The relationship between two girls and a boy
living in a small beach town on Long Island changes during
their thirteenth summer, when one girl's mother is dying of
cancer and the boy witnesses a child's drowning.
    ISBN 0-385-31074-9
    [1. Interpersonal relations—Fiction.   2. Death—Fiction.
3. Beaches—Fiction.   4. Long Island (N.Y.)—Fiction.]   I. Title.
PZ7.H7933Li   1993
[Fic]—dc20   92-43048
                                                       CIP
                                                        AC

Book Design by Gretchen Achilles

Manufactured in USA
November 1993
10   9   8   7   6   5   4   3   2   1
BVG

Many thanks to my friends and fellow writers Amy Gottfried, Trisha Lester, Jim Lindsay, Laurie Hussey, Thomas Gavin, Susan Hubbard, Mary Bush, and Chris Zenowich, and to Susan Scarfe and Wendy Lamb. Finally, thanks to Siobhan McPartlin DiZio, for suggesting Delacorte Press.

For Mom and Pop,
of course,
and for Khaled,
always

1. Life Belts

The summer we both turned thirteen, Anita Blake and I spent the end of June repairing an old sailboat not much bigger than a surfboard, and July and August sailing it up and down the coast of our Long Island village. The boat was wooden, made originally from a kit and bought secondhand by my father, who used it for a few summers and then gave it to us. By that time, he'd moved up in the world with the purchase of a fiberglass Sunfish with a cockpit he could curl up and doze in on calm days, and a rudder with a fancy extension. Our boat had neither cockpit nor fancy rudder; it was wooden, rotten to the core, and very leaky, but we captained it gladly, thrilled with the freedom it gave us. We patched the canvas sail and laid strips of fiberglass over the worn wooden seams of the boat, getting splinters of glass in our bare fingers and doing a sloppy job in spite of the care we took. Then we painted the whole thing a glossy blue. We drilled a hole in the stern and put a cork in it so that after every sail we could lift the boat from the bow and drain it. We were always surprised at how much water it sucked up, like some parched blue sea animal, no matter how briefly we'd had it out. The water poured out of the hole a dirty yellow, with chips of rotten wood floating onto the sand. We spent hours that summer standing on the shoreline, watching our boat pee.

The second the boat was seaworthy, Nita and I took it out on the water. I had already learned from my father how to sail. I knew how to feel the wind, how to angle the boat and maneuver the sail so that it caught even the slightest breeze to the best advantage. I tried to teach Nita these things, but she was much more interested in tipping the boat than really sailing it. She insisted on holding the sail and would toy with the line, lifting the boat on its edge to send it slicing precariously through the water. She'd bring us right to the brink of tipping, then let us down by easing up on the sail. She'd pull the sail in again, and we'd use our bodies to counterbalance the force of the wind until one of us teetered and we both took that final spill into the water. A giddy panic always followed, as we tried to keep our heads above water in spite of the laughter that emptied our lungs and threatened to send us to the rocky bottom of Long Island Sound.

Eventually, we'd make our way to the other side of the boat, where I'd hang on the centerboard and Nita would wait until she could reach the small railing, perhaps two inches high, that some smart designer had added to keep adults but not adolescent girls from sliding off the deck. We'd right the boat then, keeping our heads low to avoid being hit by the boom, and finally sliding onto the deck on our stomachs, exhausted, still laughing.

One night early in the summer, when both sets of parents were at a party on the Neck, Nita invited me to go skinny-dipping.

I told her it was out of the question. I couldn't even change my clothes in the girls' locker room before gym. I always took them into a booth in the bathroom and got dressed there. Nita, who'd been well-endowed since the fifth grade, said it was because I didn't have breasts yet.

"And don't make such a big deal out of it," she said. "We'll go from the boat."

I pointed out that it would be dark in about an hour, but Nita was persistent.

"Listen," she said. "We've had it out in the daytime, right? It's getting kind of old, don't you think? Imagine, sailing at night."

"I can imagine," I said, thinking about all the forms terror could take when it was tempted by two girls in a leaky boat in the dark. "I can imagine," I repeated, but she'd already hung up the phone.

By the time Nita got to my house, I was dead set against taking the boat out and, because I knew Nita so well, had prepared a list of arguments in my favor. "We can't," I began. "Remember *Jaws*?"

"That's just some stupid mechanical shark," Nita said. "You're afraid of a mechanical shark?"

"I don't think it's safe," I said. "It's dead low, and we won't be able to see the rocks."

"We know where the rocks are," Nita said. "We've seen them just about a million times before."

"What about the Carey boys?" I said, moving in desperation to my final argument. "Sometimes they take their motorboat out at night, and we don't have a light."

"They're not going to sneak up on us, stupid," Nita said. "Don't you think we can hear a motorboat? Are we deaf or something?"

I shook my head, knowing there was nothing more to say. I was only a little surprised that I'd been defeated so soon.

Nita grabbed my hand and pulled me out of the house. When we reached the shed in the front yard, she loaded me like a pack horse with the things we'd need: centerboard, rudder, and finally mast and boom, which she balanced on my shoulders.

"You carry," she said. "I'll watch for cars."

Nita ran to the road, looked both ways, and crossed, disappearing over the dunes before I'd even made it to the end of the driveway. I listened for cars, unable to turn and look because the sail would have hit the trees on either side of me.

"It's about time," Nita said when I reached her. She was sitting on the boat and had stripped down to her bathing suit. Her clothes and sneakers lay in a heap at her feet. "Hurry up," she said. "They're not going to be at that party all night."

I secretly wished my parents would come home immediately and catch us, but we both knew better. The Gottfrieds were famous for their parties. No one would be home before midnight.

I dropped everything on the ground and sat down to take off my sneakers and socks.

"You don't have your suit?" Nita said.

I shook my head. I hadn't bothered to change to my suit because I thought I could talk Nita into a night of TV and pirated vodka and orange juice.

Nita looked down the beach. "That's okay," she said. "It's going to be pitch black in about an hour, and you won't need it, anyway. Come on." She grabbed my hand again. This time I pulled away.

"Cut it out," I said.

"Cool it, Molly," she said. "You just don't recognize a good time when you see one."

Nita started tugging at the sailboat with me still on it. I got up and helped her, knowing she'd never forgive me if I didn't. Because it was low tide, we had to drag the boat about ten yards over pebbles, sand, and broken shells before it was at the water's edge. Every time we dragged it up or down the beach, the paint wore away a little more. Much of the blue had already been scraped off the bottom by the sand, and I knew it wouldn't be long before we wore away the fiberglass and were down to rotten wood again. I turned to Nita.

"I bet the boat sinks tonight," I said. "Look." I lifted the sailboat slightly and pointed to the places the paint had disappeared.

"Don't be stupid," Nita said. "We had it out yesterday, right? Did you notice any more piss than usual when we drained it?" She looked at me, scowling, and I shook my head. "Listen," she continued. "I finally think of a way we can really have a good time, and you want to ruin it."

Nita's mind was made up, and we were doomed. We couldn't even wear life belts, because Nita had banned them our first week out. Coast Guard–approved orange life preservers were obviously out of the question: they were ugly and would block our tans. And Nita had nixed the white ski belts after hers got caught on the edge of the boat when we tipped, and she just hung there, flailing her arms and legs around like a beetle on its back until I helped her down. Nita swore she'd rather be thrown violently from the boat, hit her head on the boom, and drown than get stuck up there again.

I went up the beach to get the sail, then rigged the boat, something Nita hadn't bothered to learn. When I finished, it was already pretty dark. Nita got on near the centerboard, and I pushed off, soaking my shorts before I was able to pull myself onboard. It was low tide. Nita had to hold the centerboard halfway up until we were out past the sandbar so that it wouldn't hit bottom. Every few seconds, she yelled at me to avoid a rock.

"I thought you knew this stuff," she said. "Do I have to navigate and do everything?"

The breeze was light and blowing straight onshore. I had to tack a few times before we even cleared the sandbar. Nita tried to get us going faster by pulling the sail way in, but the wind wasn't strong enough.

"That won't work," I said. "Just pull it in till it stops flapping. If you can't see it, you can hear it."

We were way past the boulder everyone called the Big Rock when Nita let go of the sail. I wasn't ready, and in spite of the weak breeze nearly fell backward into the water.

"Hey!" I yelled. I could barely see Nita where she sat toward the front of the boat. The water was pitch black, with only an occasional light from the houses onshore bouncing off its surface.

"Shh," Nita said.

We both sat quietly until the boat stopped rocking.

"Just look at us," she whispered. "Have you ever felt like this?"

I let go of the rudder and pulled my knees to my chest. We'd stopped moving, and it was easy to balance in the still night. I looked to shore. Most of the houses had their lights on, but we were too far away to see the people inside. It was a warm night, in spite of the heavy clouds that had covered the sky all day and kept the sun from setting. The clouds were wrapped around the earth like a damp blanket, and I felt safe under their cover. A car drove by occasionally, its lights riding ahead of it on the telephone wires like a silent message. When we were younger, Nita and I had thought that the lights on the wires were phone calls traveling to our neighbors' houses.

The boat rocked slightly and I looked toward Nita. She had taken off the top of her bathing suit, and I could see a flash of white from her breasts. She had her arms crossed below them and was looking down. She seemed to sense that I was staring at her, and in a moment she raised her head.

"It feels wonderful," she said, her voice soft as the breeze. "You should take off your clothes."

I shook my head. "Not yet," I said. "I like it the way I am."

"Fine," Nita whispered, looking down again.

I sat huddled on the deck for a long time. The only sounds were the lapping of the water at the sides of the boat, the flapping of the sail, and an occasional car going by, its progress marked by the thud thud thud of tires in the gaps of the concrete road.

There was a splash that made me lose my balance and grab the railing. Nita had rolled backward into the water, and I had to get down on my knees and then flat on my stomach to keep the boat from tipping. I had a hand on each railing and was lying there when Nita broke the surface nearby, laughing.

"It's wonderful!" she yelled. "Wonderful!"

I pulled myself up and peered into the water. I couldn't believe what I saw.

All around Nita's body the water glowed, as if the sea were exploring her flesh with a fluorescent light.

"Look." My voice cracked as I pointed at the water.

Nita looked down. She laughed wildly and started to tread water, creating a caldron of churning phosphorescence all around her.

"Nita!" I screamed, finding my voice again.

She stopped treading and looked up at me. "Cool," she pronounced.

"What is it?" I said.

She lifted her hand from the water and threw something at me. It landed on my thigh, cold and gooey. A white jellyfish.

They didn't sting like the red ones, but still, they weren't my favorite marine animal.

"Why do they do that?" I asked. "Why do they glow?"

Nita let her breath out in a rush, something she did when she thought someone had said something really stupid. "Don't you know anything?" she said. "They've got these amoebas, or plankton, or slime, or something all over them, that glows in the dark. But they only do it when you touch them. Haven't you ever walked on the beach at night?"

I had, but I'd always stayed away from the water, afraid of sharks, barnacles, crabs, or some wild form of sea life I hadn't yet heard of. I lifted the jellyfish from my thigh and threw it back at her. It broke to pieces before it hit the water by her bare shoulder. "I'm not going in there," I said. "No way."

"Come on, Molly," Nita said. "It's cool, I promise."

I looked around for shark fins, then back at her. "Okay," I said. "Okay." I took off my shorts, T-shirt, and finally my underwear, no easy task on a boat as stable as a pencil balanced on its point. I shivered when my clothes were off, though I hadn't been cold all day.

"I'll wait," I said weakly, sitting on the boat stark naked. "I'll wait until I'm ready." I pulled my knees to my chest again and balanced.

"You're always waiting," Nita said. "But what are you waiting for?"

As she spoke, she pulled herself up on the railing of the boat and tipped it. I tumbled into the water before I'd even had time to unclasp my hands from my knees.

The water was a shock. It wasn't cold, but it wasn't warm, either. And it was thick with jellyfish. They oozed through my fingers as I swam to the surface. They brushed against my face. I came up gasping.

Nita laughed. "Sorry, kid," she said. "It was too tempting."

I answered her with an angry splash. Nita splashed back, and the battle began. We showered each other with artilleries of jellyfish and salt water until we were both in a frenzy and the sea swirled like a whirlpool, glowing around our naked bodies.

At the time I wasn't thinking about the sea creatures who might have been drawn to the site of our battle—sharks attracted by the turbulence, giant bluefish with knife-sharp teeth mistaking our thrashing for the motions of bait fish. I had only one thing in mind: revenge on Nita. I was mad enough to drown her. But I didn't. When we'd had enough, we declared a truce and floated on our backs. The clouds had disappeared, and I was surprised to see stars. Nita had promised it would be wonderful and it really was. I felt wonderfully lost, lying weightless in the heavy darkness that surrounded us.

There's something comforting about the infinite depth of the night sky above, but the deep sea below can be terrifying. When I rolled over to look for the sailboat, I was suddenly afraid. I looked around and could barely make out the faint glow of the sail in the distance. The boat had floated away from us, or we from it, and I felt deserted, betrayed.

I splashed water at Nita, who still lay on her back. "The boat," I said, before I swam for it. She rolled onto her stomach and followed me. She must have known I was scared because she yelled "Jaws!" and grabbed at my feet whenever she could catch up.

By the time I reached the boat, I was in such a hurry to get onboard that I pulled myself up too quickly and tipped it over. I watched helplessly as the clothes fell into the water. Then I grabbed what I could and swam to the other side of the boat, heaving on the centerboard when I got there.

There's a moment as you right a boat when you're not sure your weight will be enough to do the job. I hung suspended from the centerboard forever before the board finally sank. Like a scene played back in slow motion, the boat righted itself.

Nita and I were breathless when we pulled ourselves onboard. Neither of us spoke or moved until our breathing had quieted. Then we both sat up and sorted through the pile of wet clothing. Nita found her bathing suit top and bottom and started to put them on. I shifted my weight back and forth to balance the boat, afraid of tipping again.

"This is stupid," Nita said as she shimmied into the bottoms. "It's stupid to get dressed at all."

I ignored her and searched through the clothes. "My underpants," I said. "Where are my underpants?" I separated each piece carefully: T-shirt, shorts, training bra. "Oh my God," I said. "My God."

"What's the big deal?" Nita said. "So you put on your shorts without underwear. Haven't you ever done *that* before, either?"

That summer, for the two weeks I was away at music camp, my mother had sewn my name in all my clothes—last name and first—so that I wouldn't lose anything. Those pink cotton underpants from Sears had my name sewn onto the waistband. I told Nita. She laughed.

"Ooo," she said. "Aren't they going to talk about you at school when one of the Carey boys finds them washed up onshore." She poked me in the ribs and it hurt. "You've got it made," she said. "You won't go two days without some ninth-grade boy asking you out on a date." When I didn't laugh, she put her hand on my shoulder. "Come on, kid," she said. "It's no big deal. The mechanical shark will probably eat them."

· · ·

Two days after our night sail, I called Nita in a panic. My mother was standing in the kitchen nearby, so I whispered into the receiver. "Come over—now," I said. "I think I'm dying."

"What?" Nita yelled into the phone so loud I was afraid my mother would hear. In fact, she might have, because she turned off the water she was running in the sink and looked at me.

"What, hon?" she said.

"Nothing," I said. "I was just talking to Nita. See ya," I said into the phone, and hung up.

My mother walked toward me and put her damp hand on my forehead. "You feeling okay?" she said. "You look kind of peaked."

My stomach did a somersault and left the rest of me behind. So it was true. My mother could even see it in my face. "I'm fine," I lied. "Just tired, I guess."

I pulled away from her hand and left the kitchen. I sat in the heat on the steps of the front porch and waited for Nita. My clothes were damp already, and sweat dripped down my face, arms, and legs, but I didn't want to go back inside. I didn't want my mother to guess any more than she already had. I didn't want her to worry.

When Nita arrived on her bicycle, brakes squealing, she barely had time to put down her kickstand before I was pulling her down the driveway. It was almost a hundred degrees, and the road was busy with cars heading to the public beach. I got tired of waiting to cross and ran in front of a line of them. What did I have to lose? I was dying.

The first, second, and third slammed on their brakes in succession. I looked back at the house when I reached the other side and saw my mother looking out the front window. I motioned to Nita to follow before the cars started up again and she did, staring defiantly at the drivers as she crossed.

The sand burned the soles of my feet as I ran down the beach ahead of Nita, and when I sat on the sailboat to wait for her, I could feel the heat of the sun through my cotton shorts.

"What is it?" Nita said when she caught up. She had her sneakers on, so she had no idea how hot the sand was. She stood in front of me, her shadow a shield against the sun. "You're acting weird."

I looked up at her. There were beads of sweat on her nose and her forehead. The sun was so bright it formed a halo around the wisps of hair on the top of her head. I tried to talk but started to cry instead. Each time I opened my mouth to speak, I was choked with a heavy sob. Nita soon tired of standing there and sat on the boat next to me, resting her hand on my knee. The gesture helped, and when I was silent, when my shoulders had stopped heaving, she spoke again. "You're scaring me, kid," she said. "What do you mean, you're dying?"

I looked at her and realized that she *was* scared. I should have known she'd be as scared as I was. After all, who'd go sailing with her after I died? She had never learned how. I started to cry again, thinking about how much she'd miss me.

"Stop blubbering and tell me, won't you?" she said.

I couldn't believe it. But when she found out why I was dying and realized it was her fault, she'd forget about being mad at me. She'd never forgive herself.

"Our night sail," I said finally. "We shouldn't have done that. We shouldn't have gone skinny-dipping."

"What are you talking about?" she said. "Did your parents find out?"

"No," I said.

"Then what does a silly night sail have to do with dying?"

"They're inside me," I said.

"Who?"

I whispered the awful truth. Nita had to lean forward to hear me, and I could see the whiteness between her heavy breasts, where the sun couldn't reach. I looked down at my own flat chest, thinking how now it would never have a chance. "The jellyfish," I whispered. "They entered my body and now they're inside me, killing me." I told her how that morning, I'd found a piece of one in my underwear, and another on a piece of toilet paper. I started sobbing again. My death would surely be slow and painful. "I don't feel well," I said. "My chest is sore; I'm tired." I looked up at her. "I'm dying," I said.

Nita didn't speak. She just sat there with her mouth hanging open.

"And it's all your fault for making me go sailing," I added. I hadn't realized until then how much I resented her for staying healthy while I suffered. I had resisted going out that night, while she had insisted. I was going to die, while she was going to live to be an old lady.

"Your underwear?" she said at last. "What are you talking about?" She shook her head and ran a hand through her long hair as if she were combing it. Then she stopped, and I saw a smile form on her face. I couldn't believe it. And then I realized why. *The sailboat.* She was thinking about how the sailboat would be hers and hers alone. She was thinking about how she'd take the oldest Carey brother out on it when I was gone. To show him the ropes when she didn't know a goddamn thing about the ropes herself.

"I don't see what's so funny," I said, practically yelling. All of a sudden I hated her.

"Listen," she said. She could hardly speak without laughing. "You haven't had your period yet, right?"

"Goddamn it," I yelled. "I don't see what that has to do with it." Here I was at the end of my life, and she was reminding me I hadn't even lived long enough to get my period.

"Molly," she said calmly, "cool it. I can't believe your mother never told you. I can't believe you don't know what's happening. That stuff—that goo you think is jellyfish—that's just what happens before you get your period. It means you're fertile. It means you could do it with Eddie Barnicle and have a web-fingered baby doing the breast stroke in your belly in no time." She patted my knee. "Jesus," she said. "You scared me for a while." Then she giggled. "I can't believe how absolutely stupid you are sometimes."

I sat completely still for a while. Then I put my hand on her hand. I didn't feel stupid. I felt relieved.

I breathed in deeply and looked out over the water. It was smooth as glass. There was no wind, and the smoke from the power plant nearby was rising straight up. The air was heavy, but I felt light. I was exhausted, but I wasn't dying. Nita and I would get old together, sitting on a porch some time in the future in creaky rocking chairs, laughing about the day I thought I was. "Thank God," I said, turning finally to Nita. "Thank God."

"Forget thanking *God*," Nita said. She wasn't laughing anymore. "Thank *you*. For not being sick." She pounded her fist so hard on the hollow sailboat, I thought she'd leave a hole. "I can't even sail the goddamn boat," she said, and we both started to laugh.

Then we did something we'd never done before. We hugged each other. We sat on the sailboat hugging until we heard the motor of the Carey boys' boat coming around the jetty.

As far as I know, no one ever found those underpants that summer, but I had variations on the nightmare that they were discovered, washing up onshore as I walked with my parents along the beach, floating to the surface when I was out with a boy on the sailboat. Those dreams were no less terrifying than one I remembered from a movie I'd seen, where in a killer's dreams, the hand of a dead man keeps rising to the surface of the river.

. . .

Nita didn't tell me until late August that her mother was sick, although she'd known about it all summer. The night she told me, we were sitting in front of a fire we'd built from dried eelgrass and driftwood. We'd snuck some vodka and orange juice out of my house and were drinking it from a kosher pickle jar. When we weren't drinking or talking, we sat with burning stalks of dried eelgrass hanging from our mouths, pretending to smoke.

We'd spent the night talking about the Carey boys and their friend Eddie Barnicle, all of whom seemed to have crushes on Nita, though none of them ever noticed me. Nita was trying to choose from among them, so she could pawn the others off on me. We went through the list of them, finding different reasons to reject each one. By the time we got to the last Carey brother, who was only eight years old, we were laughing uncontrollably.

"My father says the Carey boys are wild because they don't have a mother," I said between giggles. "My mother says they don't have a mother because they're wild."

Nita stopped laughing and stared at me. I stared back, sure by the look on her face that we'd had too much to drink.

"My mother's dying, Molly," she said. "Do you think that's why I'm so wild?"

"What?" I said, suddenly quiet.

"I'm not allowed to tell anyone," Nita said. "I promised I wouldn't. She said if I told you, you'd tell your mother. She doesn't want any sympathy." She looked at me, worried. "You wouldn't tell, would you?"

I shook my head. "What's the matter with her?"

"Lymphoma," Nita said. She didn't say anything more, but she didn't need to. The strange word sounded like death to me.

"Can't they save her?" I said, but my voice sounded tiny, insignificant.

"They can't," Nita said. She was hugging her knees to her chest, looking down, as if this hugging would protect her. "All they can do is feed her chemicals and shoot her with radiation to make her feel a lot sicker and live a little longer. She's tired of it. She won't even eat anymore. She says nothing tastes good." She rolled a stalk of eelgrass back and forth between her thumb and forefinger. It was still lit, and I thought she might burn herself, but I didn't say anything. "My father's stopped eating, too," she said. "He sits at the table across from her and plays with his food. They don't even talk anymore during dinner. And my brother and I just sit there. It's awful. Dinnertime is awful."

I threw my eelgrass cigarette into the fire and watched it catch, then burn to ash. Nita stayed quiet until I looked up.

"I'm sorry," she said. "I shouldn't have told you. But it's too much, really. Every chance my mother gets, she sits me down. 'When I'm gone,' she says, like she's going on some stupid trip. Then she sorts through her things and asks me what I'd like to take now, before her sisters get ahold of everything. 'Nothing,' I say. 'I'm not going to take anything.'"

Nita threw her eelgrass into the fire, too, and we both watched it burn. "And every time we talk," she said, "she starts to cry and tells me to hold her. She says what she'll miss most, after my father, is the way I always hug her before I go to bed at night." Nita raised a sandy hand and tried to wipe away the stream of tears that ran down her face. "I'll miss it, too," she said. "She acts as if this is only happening to her. What about us? We'll never be able to sit together at the table again." She put her head back down on her knees and was silent for a while. Then she looked up. "I wish she'd just goddamn get it over with and die," she said, but as soon as she'd spoken, a look of horror came over her face. "Oh my God," she said.

I slid close to Nita and put my arm around her shoulder,

pulling her close to comfort her. When I did, her whole body went stiff. I looked from Nita to the dying fire. I let go and moved away. We sat like that forever, side by side but far apart, until all that was left was smoldering ash. Then Nita stood up, wiped the sand from her shorts, and walked away.

"I'll see you," she said from somewhere near the beach grass, already far away from me in the darkness.

2. Turbulence

Eddie Barnicle got up before sunrise to meet the Carey boys on the beach by six. They'd called the night before, excited because they'd found a clamming boat that had washed up onshore in the last storm. The boat had no registration numbers, they told him, and that made it theirs. If Eddie would bring his clamming rake, they could spend the whole day out on the water.

Of course, Eddie knew he wouldn't spend five minutes on the water if his mother had anything to say about it. There'd be too many questions: *Does their father know? Is one of the older boys going with you? Will you wear life belts? Whose boat is it?* By the time he'd satisfied her with his answers, the Carey boys would have left without him.

He fumbled for his cutoffs in the dark, then snuck down the hall past his parents' bedroom door. He left a note on the kitchen table telling them where he'd be and went out the sliding doors into the backyard to get the clamming rake he and his father had found on the beach in the spring. It should have been hanging from the crooked limb of a dogwood tree, but it must have fallen in the last storm, the same storm that had washed the Carey boys' new boat to shore. Eddie picked it up off the dew-covered lawn, noticing how rusty the teeth were, how old the wood looked. Still, it was the only rake they had, and it would have to do.

It was chilly in the shade as Eddie started down the road. An orange glow filtered through the woods across the street, and he hurried, hoping to get a glimpse of the sun as it came up over the water. He could see the Careys' house in the distance when he reached the bottom of the hill, where the trees ended and the beach began. It was the oldest and the biggest on the strip—three stories—and was made of stone. Across the street from the front yard was the Sound, and in the backyard, down an incline and beyond a stack of railroad ties, the bay began, all muck and stink at low tide, but filled when the tide was high with warm brown water the boys swam in all the way through September.

Eddie left the sandy shoulder of the road and climbed one of the dunes on the Sound side to get a better look at the sunrise. He was never up to see it, and now he was struck by its beauty. He'd visited the beach nearly every day this summer, but it had never looked like this. The silhouettes of two fishermen standing motionless near the jetty seemed painted onto the landscape, and the landscape itself was transformed. Even the power plant, whose red and white smokestacks slashed the shoreline like ugly scars in the daytime, looked regal in the morning light.

He could tell by the look of the sun that the day would be a scorcher. That was the way August was on Long Island. In August, storms hit that blew so hard and lasted so long, everyone was sure that the summer was over, and then, maybe even the next day, the sun would be so hot you'd feel the wind had blown you back in time to the middle of July or forward to October, when Indian summer hit and guys who'd spent the real summer living wild, running shirtless and barefoot, drinking beers in the sand dunes or behind bushes in the public park now sat behind desks—shoes too tight, shirt buttoned too high—in the stifling heat of a dismal brick building.

Sea gulls were squawking down the beach, and Eddie saw them hovering and diving near the Big Rock, which, near midtide, was just beginning to show above the water. Nearby he noticed a turbulence of baitfish thrashing at the surface, trying to escape the sharp teeth of the blues that fed below. *Boy, do those blues feed,* Eddie thought. Once, surf-casting with his father, he'd gotten a hit so big his pole had bent nearly in half with the strain of it, but when he got the fish to shore, all that was left was the head of a mossbunker, its jaw still clamped around the hook, pieces of its gut trailing behind.

There was another disturbance a little closer to shore, and Eddie thought he saw someone swimming, though with the glare of the sun off the water, he couldn't be sure. He slid down the dune to get a better look.

It *was* someone—a woman or a girl with long blond hair that trailed behind her as she swam. He wondered if she'd seen the blues feeding. If she had, she was crazy. They weren't picky eaters. They'd bite at anything. But she had nearly reached the shore, and Eddie knew there was no need to worry now.

He had already started toward the Careys' beach when he realized that the swimmer was Anita Blake, a girl in the eighth grade, a girl everyone he knew—including all the Carey brothers —would die for. She reached the shore and rose from the sea— naked, skin glistening—and Eddie stood transfixed. He put his left hand behind him and tried to make himself invisible, but he felt like an ugly blotch on the landscape that had only a moment ago seemed so beautiful.

Eddie knew it was ridiculous to hide his hand when he stood so far from her. And hiding it didn't make the webs of skin that joined three of his fingers go away. When he was younger, his mother had sat him in her lap and examined the webs, which were blue-veined and thin like paper, as if they were something of great value, a miracle.

His mother thought his hand made him special, but Eddie knew it only made him different. He'd found that out as soon as he'd started school. His hand made it difficult to have friends. It made teachers treat him differently, because of the great care they took *not* to treat him differently. Now, after a year in junior high school, his hand was something to hide whenever he got near a girl—and he was obsessed with girls. All around him, they were blossoming in ways that could keep him awake at night if he thought too hard about them. Even Anita Blake's friend Molly, who was flat-chested and plain-looking, was beginning to appeal to him. He knew there was no way he'd ever get any girl to go out with him, not the way his hand looked, and Anita Blake wasn't just any girl. He could stop thinking about her right now.

But he couldn't stop staring.

Anita walked up the beach to her towel, and though Eddie couldn't move, though he could hardly breathe, he followed her closely with his eyes. She was pale where her bathing suit should have been, dark everyplace else. She was soft. She was graceful. She was smooth, and hard, and taut.

When Anita looked his way Eddie scrambled over the sand dunes, tripping over the rake when it caught in the beach grass. He'd stop thinking about her, he told himself as he struggled to stand. He'd stop right this minute.

"What took you?" Trevor Carey said when Eddie ran down the path to their beach. He had thick black hair, and on his tanned face were the beginnings of a beard that made his face look constantly dirty. His younger brother Robbie, a scrawny blond boy who looked as if he belonged in grade school, added, "Yeah. What took you?"

Eddie shrugged and dropped the rake into the bottom of the boat. "Couldn't find the rake," he said, wanting to keep the vision of Anita to himself.

"Well, come on," Trevor said. "Help us get this thing in the water." He went to the front of the boat to pull from the bow, and Eddie joined Robbie at the stern. Even with the three of them pulling and pushing, the boat moved slowly. It was wooden, and probably waterlogged. Attached to the stern between Eddie and Robbie was a small five-horsepower motor, hardly enough to move a boat this heavy through the water, but at least better than rowing the long stretch around the Neck to the bay where they would clam. The old wood was covered with a new coat of gray paint, except at one place on the bow, where the registration numbers should have been. There the paint was scraped away and bare wood showed, as if the bow had run against a rock.

As they pushed the boat into the water, Eddie worried that Anita would still be on the beach. He tried to waste time taking off his sneakers, but Trevor soon lost patience. He ordered Eddie into the boat and he obeyed, reluctantly taking a seat at the bow.

Eddie soon realized that the Careys weren't interested in the shoreline at all. They kept their eyes on the baitfish that shattered the glassy surface of the water every few minutes, the feeding blues beneath them throwing them into a frenzy. Eddie tried to join in by pointing out possible schools far out on the horizon, and when they were well beyond the Big Rock, he snuck a look toward shore.

The beach was a sandy blank slate.

. . .

By the time the boys reached the bay side, the air was thick with humidity and the sun was beating down hard. It had taken them longer than it should have to get around the point because they'd chased schools of bluefish the whole way, zigzagging in the water in whatever direction they saw gulls and turbulence. But the small motor was so noisy and so slow that the fish always disappeared beneath the surface before they reached them.

Trevor cut the motor and they drifted awhile before Eddie dropped anchor. It must have been well past eight o'clock, but there were no other boats in the inlet. The houses onshore, too, looked deserted—except the Devin house, where a small child sat at the top of the long sloping lawn and stared at the water.

"Hand me a beer, will you?" Trevor said.

Eddie reached for a line at the front of the boat and pulled it in. They had rigged a net to hold two six-packs, and the beer had dangled in the water, cooling off, as they made their way to the inlet. Eddie was sure the boys had stolen the beer from either their father or their oldest brother, who always had six-packs stashed in the trunk of his car. He handed a can to each of them and then took one for himself.

Eddie felt good, his outsides warmed by the sun, insides cooled by the beer. All summer, they'd borrowed the boys' oldest brother's boat to cruise along the shore, but they could only use it when he didn't want it and lately, because of his new girlfriend, he wanted it all the time. Now they had their own boat, to take out when they pleased. Eddie leaned back against the wooden bow and breathed the smells around him: new paint, salt air, and August heat. He closed his eyes and thought about Anita Blake, letting the sun caress his face. He didn't care if they got any clams at all today. It was worth it just to be sitting here.

When the boys had finished their beers, Trevor grabbed the

clamming rake. Now the heavy work would begin, and every beer they drank from now on would have to be earned. He worked the rake quickly through the muck on the bottom. He was strong, Eddie thought. The rake didn't seem at all heavy in his hands. When he brought it to the surface, it was filled with an oozy black muck and about half a dozen cherrystone clams. Four of the clams were keepers.

Robbie worked the rake the next time, and after a long struggle, he came up with only a spider crab and a few mussels. He swore and dumped them back, and then it was Eddie's turn. He dragged the rake through the muck on the other side of the boat, the side the Careys hadn't touched yet. At first it stuck, but he struggled to scoop up some of the bottom while the boys helped balance the boat. The rake was almost too heavy, and he tried not to grunt as he lifted it from the water and rested the long handle on the edge of the boat. He was used to the smell of the muck now, even savored it. Twice a day, for as long as he could remember, this smell had hung over the village at low tide like a haze, overpowering in the summer, sharp but fleeting in the winter. It was the smell of seaweed, dead shellfish, and rotting vegetation—but something else, too. For years Eddie had used it to tell the time and the tide. If time had a smell, Eddie thought, this was it.

Mud, fiddler crabs, and mussels fell through the mesh when Eddie jiggled the rake. Only one cherrystone remained, but when he took it from the rake and rinsed it, the clam felt substantial in his hand. He tossed it into the bottom of the boat alongside Trevor's catch, noting with satisfaction that his was bigger than any of the other four clams.

When there were a couple of dozen clams in the bottom of the boat, the boys took a break. They drank beer while Trevor shucked clams with his Swiss army knife. Eating clams fresh from the bottom of the bay was almost a religious experience, and the boys did it in silence. As he ate, Eddie concentrated again on Anita, on the way she'd looked coming out of the water.

It was getting hotter, and Eddie decided to take off his shirt. The beer had made him dizzy, and he had trouble balancing as he pulled it over his head. When he draped the shirt on the seat beside him, he noticed that Trevor had put his knife down and taken his off as well. He was only four months older than Eddie and less than a year older than Robbie, but he had the body of a muscular man, the kind of body that would get all the attention of the girls when they went back to school. Trevor was much bigger now, at the end of the summer, than he'd been at the beginning.

Robbie handed Eddie an open shell, and Eddie raised it to his lips to suck out the clam, eyeing Trevor jealously. Robbie handed him another, and Eddie drained the shell quickly, letting the clam rest for a moment on his tongue before sending it on its way. It slithered smoothly down his throat and left a taste he was greedy for. Its saltiness made his mouth water. No matter how quickly he ate, though, Eddie noticed that Trevor seemed to eat two clams to his one. He was surprised that this bothered him, but it did. For some reason he pictured the boy's muscular arm around Anita's soft damp shoulder and felt slightly sick.

He looked away from Trevor toward the Devin house, where on the sloping lawn the small child had begun to whirl herself round and round with her arms flung wide. Her white dress floated up and around her like a haze, and she fell dizzily, getting up quickly, only to begin again. With each spin, she landed a little farther from the house, a little closer to the water.

In a while Eddie noticed that the Carey boys, too, were watching, though no one spoke. When a fish jumped behind them, all three turned quickly to look.

"Should've brung the poles," Robbie said.

"Yeah," his brother answered. Then to Eddie: "Hand me another beer, will you, Frog?"

"Yeah, Froggy," Robbie echoed. "Make that two."

The Careys had given him that name in grade school when they'd discovered that his fingers were webbed. It hadn't bothered Eddie in years, but today he resented it. He shook the two cans slightly before handing them to Robbie. Robbie passed one to his brother, and Eddie thought he saw Trevor's muscles bulge as he pulled off the flip-top. The beer sprayed out of the opening and foamed down his arm, but he didn't seem to notice. He drained the can quickly, crushing it in his hand. Then he threw the empty container overboard. It landed lightly on the surface and rocked back and forth, taking on water through the hole in the top until it sank. "Gotta piss," the boy said.

"Me, too," his brother said, balancing the full beer can awkwardly on the seat beside him.

Trevor pointed to a piece of seaweed floating in the water. "Try for that," he told Robbie. "Bet you can't make it."

"Bullshit," Robbie said. He was redfaced, either from the heat or from the beer. He unzipped his shorts and stood unsteadily. He peed in spurts that drizzled into the water far short of the target. Then he zipped his shorts back up and sat down, picking up his beer can and peering into it without speaking.

"What about you, Edboy?" Trevor said. "Can you make it?"

Eddie's bladder was so full, he thought he could pee to Connecticut and back. "Sure," he said. "No problem." He waited for Trevor to go first. The longer he waited, the better distance he'd get.

"We'll go together," Trevor said after a moment. "You go from that end and I'll go from this." He stood at the back of the boat.

Because his swimming trunks had no zipper, he had to pull them down. His pubic hair was as black and as coarse as the beard on a mussel shell. Eddie unzipped his own shorts and turned slightly away. His hair was still sparse and fine.

"You tell us when to start," Trevor said to his brother.

On a cue from Robbie, they both peed, but for some reason Eddie couldn't aim. His stream crossed beneath Trevor's and landed in a trickle miles away from the seaweed. He sat down quickly, afraid of losing his balance. Trevor hit the target straight on, and the seaweed soon sank beneath a gush of yellow.

"The Frog's drunk as a fish," Trevor said, laughing and pulling up his shorts.

"Am not," Eddie said defiantly.

"Oh, yeah?" the younger brother said, no longer staring into his beer can, reveling instead in the family victory. "Bullshit."

"I was thinking about something else," Eddie said. "Something a lot more interesting than pissin' in the stinkin' bay."

"What were you thinking about, Edboy?" Trevor said.

When Eddie considered describing the way Anita had looked coming out of the water, he could no longer see her clearly. He worried that if he tried to describe what he'd seen, he wouldn't be able to picture her at all. "You wouldn't believe it," he said finally, sorry that he'd brought her up, sorry he was in the boat with the boys at all.

"Sure we would, Frog," Trevor said. "We'd believe anything you told us. You're too much of a wimp to lie."

"Yeah," his brother said. "Tell us."

"Anita Blake," Eddie said. "I saw Anita Blake on my way to your beach."

"So?" Trevor said.

"She was naked," Eddie answered.

"Bullshit," Robbie said.

"It's true," Eddie said. "She was skinny-dipping. I was up on the dunes, looking at the sunrise. She came right out of the water like she didn't care if anyone saw her or not."

"Keep dreamin', Frog," Trevor said.

"Bullshit," Robbie said.

"Anyway, who cares?" Trevor spit into the water and his spit floated on the surface like scum. "She doesn't go out with am*phibi*ans."

"Yeah," Robbie said. He grabbed his gut and laughed. "*Amphibians.*"

Eddie reached for the collar of the younger boy's shirt and twisted it. "Take it back," he said. Robbie looked up at him with bulging eyes and made a gurgling sound, too drunk to defend himself. Trevor grabbed Eddie's hair and yanked it until Eddie let go. The two boys stood facing each other near the middle of the boat while Robbie sat unsteadily between them.

"Forget it," Eddie said. The boat was rocking violently, and it was all he could do to remain standing. "I was lying, if that's what you want to believe." When he said it, he felt relieved, as if he'd reclaimed Anita for himself. Trevor stared at him for a long time, unblinking, and then they both sat down.

When the boat had stopped rocking, Trevor picked up the rake and started to clam again. Eddie looked away from him toward the Devin house, where the girl in the white dress still twirled. She had nearly reached the dock.

"Holy shit," the Carey boys said together. Eddie turned to see that Trevor had skewered a toadfish with one of the rake's rusty prongs. Its fins and feelers hung from its body like cancerous red growths. It opened its huge mouth in a silent scream and wriggled, as if in wriggling it could swim away.

"Ever seen one that big?" Trevor said to Eddie. He was holding it over the inside of the boat, dripping mud and fish blood onto the boat's floor.

Eddie studied the fish carefully. Its eyes were glazed like the eyes of a very old man, its teeth jutted from its gums like shards of glass, and its jaw was enormous, maybe six inches across. These fish used their jaws to crush the shells of oysters and other shell-fish, and some people called them oyster crushers, but Eddie knew they could take a toe or a finger off if it got in the way. He'd caught a few near the Big Rock when he was fishing for blackfish or flounder, and they were always ugly, but this one was so big and so hideous, it seemed to be rotting in front of his eyes.

"No way," he said. "Not that big."

Robbie slapped his brother on the back while Trevor moved the rake back and forth in his hand so that the prong twisted in the bright orange belly of the fish. Then he turned the rake over, and the toadfish flopped into the bottom of the boat near Eddie.

"He's about dead by now," Robbie said, disappointed. He lifted the fish by its tail, but his brother stopped him.

"Keep it," he said. "We oughta get it stuffed."

"Yeah," Robbie answered, laughing. "Stuff it."

There was a loud splash by the Devin house. The three boys turned to look. Eddie thought maybe the blues would start jump-ing, but there were no more disturbances. If it was a fish that had jumped, it was in no hurry to jump again. He looked at one Carey boy and then the other, but neither of them returned his gaze. Their eyes were fixed on a point off the end of the Devin dock where rings in the water spread, diminished, and disappeared.

Eddie remembered the girl in the white dress. She was no-where in sight. She must have gone back inside the house, he told himself. She was probably at her kitchen table right now, telling her mother about the boat out on the bay. The gray one with the three boys in it.

He sat with the Carey boys and watched until the water was once again as smooth as the rest of the bay.

3. Tunnel

the Sound was cold because of a recent rain storm, and Nita swam fast, first to get warm, then for the pleasure of it. She liked to swim naked, and the only time to do that was around sunrise. Everyone in the whole damn town was too lazy to be up except for a few ancient fishermen, and if one of them saw her, who cared? She might distract him, the tide might rise and fill his waders as he stood, gaping helplessly at her incredible beauty, but he'd drown happy, that's for sure. She'd give the old man what was due him. What was due everyone. A happy death. An incredibly happy ending to a story as sad or as dull or as wicked as his silly life.

The water rushed like inquisitive hands down her body, probed a cold finger between her breasts. She pushed herself, swam even faster, until her muscles ached with the effort. Then she thought about her mother, who lay in bed at home, dying slowly, making the whole thing as unhappy as any death could be. When Nita held her, her shoulders were as frail and brittle as the shed of a calico crab. If she lost herself in a moment of closeness, if she squeezed too tightly, Nita knew her mother would crumble and turn to dust. It was that simple. It was that sad.

Nita remembered the day her father had taken her out on the beach to tell her. In the past, they'd always gone on walks together as a family, though Denny had been distant these past few months, ever since he'd begun growing that scrawny beard, had started caring more about his stupid car than about anyone in the family. He lay under it daily, like a faithful lover. It was sick.

So this spring and summer there had been fewer walks. Her parents still took them, but they seemed to want to walk alone. She'd seen them often from Molly's beach or from the jetty, holding hands and heading toward the Neck. She'd keep her eyes on them until they were like two specks of dust near the point. If she looked away, she was never able to find them again.

That was why, when her father had asked her to walk with him near the beginning of the summer and her mother hadn't even offered to come along (she was too tired, she said), Nita knew something was wrong.

They walked for a long time in silence toward the point, where she'd seen her parents walk so many times. Then her father stopped and took her hand.

When he did, she wanted to run away. They're getting a divorce, she thought. Mom didn't come along because they're getting a divorce and this is the way they've decided to tell me. She hadn't noticed that they weren't getting along, just that they seemed unhappy, but this was what friends at school had told her it was like. They tried to protect you, tried to pretend they liked each other for the sake of the children, then they hit you with the news like it was some deadly, destructive bomb. It fell from the air with no warning and landed where, a moment before, there had been the illusion of a constant, seamless peace. Nita closed her eyes, as if not seeing the damage—in the new lines on her father's face, the new expression in his eyes—would keep it from being real.

"This is a terrible thing," her father said.

Nita kept her eyes closed, waiting for him to say more, but he didn't speak. As the silence passed, she began to feel sorry for the man, sorry for him even as she hated him for what he and her mother were about to do. "Just say it," she said finally. "Say it."

"Your mother," he said, and paused. Nita looked up at him, anticipating the rest: *Your mother and I are getting a*—but he interrupted her thought. "She's very ill," he said. "She's dying."

Nita didn't speak for a while, trying to absorb what her father had said. She realized she was angry—angry at her father for saying what he'd just said so calmly, and angry at her mother for letting it be so. Even now, weeks later, she kicked and slapped at the water as if to do it damage, but only put herself in pain.

"Can't they help her?" she said finally, though as she spoke she had no idea who *they* were, still had no idea who *they* were—just people, she imagined, who in the end would do to her mother what they'd done to her grandmother: put her in a hospital bed, stick her with tubes, and drain the life out of her in liquids red and clear.

Her father had told her no, had explained that her mother had cancer, lymphoma, that they (he used the word, too, didn't even say doctors, just *they*) were trying a few things, would continue to try a few things so that she'd live longer, but really, it was too far along. He was telling her, he said, because her mother had wanted it that way, because her mother couldn't do it herself.

Nita swam faster, pushed harder, until her lungs burned. It was funny, she thought. They'd finished their walk, hadn't turned around until they'd made it all the way to the point and stuck their feet in the water. As they walked she imagined them shrinking until they disappeared into the millions of grains of sand along the beach. If her mother came out searching, even if she searched all night and through the next day, she'd never find them. They'd leave her long before she ever got the chance to leave them.

They stood at the point a long time, knee-deep in the water, not talking. Nita heard a single gull crying in the distance. She could feel a steady stream of tears running down her face, though she'd been trying all along not to cry. Her father stood beside her, not speaking, not even looking at her, though at one point he rested his hand on her shoulder. She remembered being surprised at how heavy that hand was, how it seemed to want to push her under.

The water was still cold then. It was June, and they'd had a rainy cold spell before the summer had gotten a chance to take hold. Perhaps it was the weight of her father's hand, perhaps she dove in to kick off the ache that had begun in her knees. What-ever the cause, she found herself swimming straight out, her shorts and gauzy shirt rubbing against her body, chafing her skin like chapped or calloused hands. Her father called her, but his voice soon faded to nothing.

If she was crying, she was no longer aware of it because she could no longer feel the tears. Soon all she was aware of was her own labored breathing, the burning in her lungs, and the ache of her muscles—every muscle, it seemed, in her body. When she could swim no farther, she stopped and looked to shore, but couldn't see her father anywhere. She was afraid he had aban-doned her—had gone home to her mother, or worse—had gone underwater and decided he liked it on the rocky bottom, with its otherworldly terrain, its silence so constant, so complete, it was deafening.

Then he broke the surface near her, shot out of the water like a rocket, yelling "Woo-eee!" and again, "Woo-eee!" and laughing his crazy laugh. "Good idea, Anita Blake," he said. "That was a damned good idea." He splashed her and she splashed back, and for a few minutes they both forgot that anything was wrong with the world.

When they dragged themselves out of the water, the illusion wore off. What her father had told her was a fact. She could read it on his face when he joined her on the beach. She could read it in the beach, with its sad silent welcome. Even the gull was gone.

On the way back, her father kept his eyes down, scanning the high-tide mark. It was clearly delineated as far as Nita could see by a line of shells and seaweed about two feet wide. At one time, mostly jingle shells and scallop shells had littered the beach. Now there were mostly mussel shells, some blue, some more black than blue, all with remnants of beards from the time they lived and clung to something solid, something stationary. Some were lying singly, some in pairs, the waves and the weight of beachcombers having not yet broken that small bit of shell that bonded them.

Nita thought the mussels made the beach look dirty. The line they left looked like an oil spill, the kind the power plant seemed to have at the beginning of every summer so that even though the company sent men with dark tans in huge dump trucks to clean up the beach, Nita and Molly would often go home with gobs of oil between their toes or stuck to the bottoms of their feet.

Nita's father stopped and held out his hand to show Nita a crushed mussel with the animal still inside. Pieces of it thrust through the broken shell, and Nita smelled its rotting shellfish smell on the breeze. He picked at the mussel, lifting a bit of shell to expose more of the inside. "You see this?" he said, poking at the meat, the stomach, the gooey remains. "This is life, the life of the mussel." He dug his fingernail into the fish and pushed some of it away to expose the white part that looked like a baby's tooth and clung to the shell, the part that kept the two halves sealed when alive. "This is the muscle that keeps these two halves together, keeps the life inside." He dropped the mussel and wiped his hand on his shorts, then reached down to retrieve another—long dead, flesh no longer clinging to its hard shell. The two halves were still joined, though, spread like angel's wings. The outside of the shells was worn, the blueness crusty with black and bits of dried seaweed, but the inside was white and shiny, like a freshwater pearl.

"This is what's important about life," he said, rubbing his finger over the smooth whiteness. "Because it endures beyond the flesh, and because it's beautiful. It doesn't last, but it always—always—leaves something beautiful behind."

He stared at the shell for a while, then looked at Nita. "Remember that," he said, putting his hand on Nita's cheek to caress it. "Whatever you do, always remember that."

She nodded, but as she did she wondered where all the bright-colored jingle shells were, once so numerous, with a sheen like the mica in the rocks along the jetty. Then she realized that an abundance of certain shells only meant that those shellfish were dying more quickly than all the others. Years ago, it was the scallops and jingles that were dying. This year, it was the mussels. Maybe she should appreciate them. Maybe after this summer, she'd never see a mussel shell again.

Today the water made Nita's skin tingle, but it wasn't cold. It was exhilarating—that's what her mother would say. Or refreshing. The water was refreshing. Before her illness, Nita's mother had had a positive thing to say about everything, every situation, but now she was always unhappy. Even when she tried to hide it, Nita could tell by the way she carried herself, the way she picked things up—objects around the house, maybe a photograph, a piece of pottery she'd made—and then put them down suddenly, as if they caused her some deep pain. If she noticed Nita watching her, she'd smile and make some halfhearted comment or other, but she no longer seemed to feel the things she said. All she felt was this pain that colored everything in the house. Every*one* in the house, too. Nita had often caught her mother staring at her as if she were already gone, as if her daughter already existed in some distant, irretrievable past.

And her father was no better. After that day, Nita noticed the pairs of shells that he left around the house. She'd find them everywhere—her parents' bedside table, the telephone table, the soap dish in the bathroom—all connected. Some were the shells of razor clams, some mussels, cherrystones, angel wings. Occasionally she'd even find two jingle shells joined—shiny, golden, like a promise. If they broke apart, she removed them and threw them away. Neither of her parents ever mentioned them, yet there they were, more numerous every day, as if even in death they had the power to multiply and no one in the house had the power to stop them.

Nita stopped swimming and looked around, sculling the water with her hands to keep from sinking. She was out way past the Big Rock, farther than she'd ever been before—except when she was sailing with Molly, of course. *Molly* would think she was being too daring. *Molly* thought that you should swim parallel to the shoreline, should never go out too far over your head. What was the difference, Nita wanted to know, if you were a little over your head or a lot over your head? Didn't people drown at home in their own bathtubs? Hadn't old people and little kids been known to fall face down and drown in two-inch-deep puddles? Molly was a prude and a coward, that was all Nita knew.

And let's not forget stupid. Molly was that, too. When Nita had told her about her mother a few nights ago, Molly had responded with silence. And when she had put her hand on Nita's shoulder, as if she alone had the power to make things right again, well, Nita wouldn't stand for that at all. Molly didn't know anything. She didn't even know what the hell was going on in her own body. If she couldn't recognize her period when it was on its way, how the hell could she pretend to know anything about death?

Nita hadn't seen Molly since that night. Molly hadn't called Nita, and Nita hadn't bothered to call Molly. What was the use? Molly would be uncomfortable if Nita talked about her mother, and Nita would be uncomfortable if she didn't. Was she supposed to pretend this terrible thing wasn't happening? Did Molly think if she ignored it, it would go away? Well, good luck to her, if that was what she thought. Wait until she got her first cramps, if that was what she thought.

Nita held her body stiff and let herself sink. To hell with Molly, she told herself. To hell with everyone. She pushed the water up with her hands to force herself to the bottom. As her hair rose above her, she imagined it as a comet's tail, burning bright and beautiful, but consuming the comet as its beauty grew. She pushed the water again and sank deeper. Beneath her was blackness, while above her she could see the rays of the sun, refracted, trying in vain to light the dark underworld. Her lungs ached, but she struggled to stay down, pushing the water above and away from her. She wanted to touch the bottom with her feet. She wanted to grab on to a rock and stay down there, see what it was like. She wanted to be able to stay underwater without pain, without panic, her mind empty, only the sounds of the sea around her. She listened, and as she listened she thought that drowning must be wonderful. She was sure it must be wonderful to sink forever into this heavy black silence.

Then Nita's lungs exploded and the air rushed out of them. They were two empty sacks when she finally broke the surface of the water, gasping for breath. They were two empty sacks that wouldn't stay empty. They were hungry for air. She fed them, gulping in air as if she herself were starved for it, when all she had really wanted was to stay underwater, suspended in time, suspended in space, weightless.

Nita floated on her back, her mind a blank until the sound of sea gulls squawking somewhere farther out brought her back. She rolled over and looked in the direction of their cries, but the sun was too bright for her to see them. They were probably excited about a school of blues or something. It didn't take much to get a gull excited. Just let a slimy fish jump out of the water, and they practically had a cow.

She looked toward shore and started in the direction of the Big Rock. There were two fishermen on the beach to the left of the jetty, but they didn't seem to notice her. Hardcore fishermen —the kind that got up before sunrise—never noticed anything. They weren't like the tourists or the little kids, who had a fit every time they landed even the tiniest baitfish. If a hardcore fisherman caught ten striped bass, well, fine. If not, he'd be back the next morning anyway. And they didn't even *talk* to each other, for godsakes.

When she had nearly reached the Big Rock, Nita stopped swimming and floated on her back to rest. The gulls were nearer now, and she listened to their raucous sounds as she caught her breath. Her muscles were sore from swimming so far, but it was a good kind of pain—not like her mother's.

Nita rolled onto her stomach and swam toward shore. When she knew she could touch bottom, she lowered her feet and stood up. She liked this part the best, coming out of the water after a long swim. She took long strides. Her skin tingled as if it were brand-new, as if her early morning swim had washed off all the old skin and replaced it with skin more beautiful, but tougher, too. Even the water, for all its power, couldn't permeate her new skin. It beaded up like tiny silver balls, then rolled off her. That ball, there, that was lymphoma, that one her father's strange behavior, and that, Denny's desertion of her. But soon her old skin would return, her body would weigh her down, and she'd realize that nothing had changed. She'd walk up the beach to where she kept her towel and clothes. She'd dress quickly so that she could hurry home to be there when her parents got up.

As she approached the high-tide mark, Nita looked up the beach and realized she was being watched. The moment she did, web-fingered Eddie Barnicle turned and bolted, tripping over the clamming rake he held in his hands like an awkward weapon. She grabbed her towel and wrapped it around her body. Then she watched him scramble on his knees in the beach grass, dragging the rake behind him.

It was ruined, she thought. Her ritual was ruined. How many days had Eddie watched her before? And the Carey boys, too. She was sure they'd been there. They'd probably slipped over the dunes just before Eddie did. Eddie Barnicle couldn't even take a piss without the Carey boys nearby, hanging on to his free hand.

The house looked desolate as Nita walked up the driveway. The rock garden out front was full of weeds, and the steps to the front door were unswept. A small pile of dead leaves on the middle of the first step caught the hot breeze as she approached, swirling round and round in a morbid, manic dance.

When Nita closed the screen door behind her, she saw her mother at the top of the stairs. She had on a blue cotton bathrobe that hung from her bony shoulders like something ten sizes too big. She was leaning on the wall for support, swaying slightly, as if she were drunk. "What's going on, honey?" she said, the sound of her voice more like an echo than the real thing.

Nita stared at her for a long time before she answered. She realized that her mother, who stood at the top of the stairs as if at the end of a long dark tunnel, was slowly disappearing.

"Nothing," she said. "Absolutely nothing."

4. Weeds

The air grew heavy, the silence more intense, as Eddie watched the still place on the water. The whole bay was smooth, as it had been all morning, but the water off the end of the Devin dock looked more still, more lifeless, than the rest.

"Let's get out of here," Trevor said.

"Maybe we can save her," Eddie said.

"Save her? Save who? I didn't see anything, did you?" Trevor said this to his younger brother, who had no answer for him until he leaned over him, dark and threatening as a storm cloud.

"Nope," Robbie croaked. His face was red again, as if he were about to cry. His eyes were wide, his hands white-knuckled as they gripped the wooden seat beneath him. "I didn't see a thing." He turned to Eddie, and both boys stared at him, waiting for him to agree.

"She might have gone under," Eddie said. "Did you see her go back to the house? Did she make that splash? Did she go under?"

He could already see their pictures on the front page of the *Observer*. "Teenage Boys Save Child After Tumble into Bay," the headline would read. "Eddie Barnicle: Teenage Hero," it would say in smaller print. That because he would be the one to dive from the boat, the one to swim to the bottom and free the girl from the weeds. If necessary, he'd perform mouth-to-mouth resuscitation. The Carey boys probably didn't even know what mouth-to-mouth resuscitation was. He was excited now and stood, rocking the boat, threatening to tip it over.

"Listen, Eddie," Trevor said. His voice cut through the dense heat like an oar through water. "I didn't see anything."

"Come on, start the motor," Eddie said. "We only have four minutes," he added, remembering that from somewhere.

"I'll start the motor," Trevor said. "I'll start the motor so we can get the hell out of here." He pulled the starter rope with a force that made Eddie fall back onto his seat. The motor sputtered, then died. He pulled it again. The motor coughed. The smell of gasoline filled the air. But this time the motor kept running. Trevor let it idle, and Eddie watched as a slick of gas floated away from the boat. It caught the sun and gave back the colors of the rainbow.

"We have to save her," Eddie said.

"That's a great idea, Frog," Trevor yelled over the sound of the motor. "What if she didn't fall in? What if she's in the house, and we go over there and make a big deal out of looking for her?" He pointed to the beer cans on the floor of the boat. "What about these?" he asked. "And what about clamming without a license? And where the hell do you think this boat came from, anyway? God? That's a great idea."

"What do you mean, where'd the boat come from?" Eddie yelled back. "We found it."

Trevor looked at his younger brother and laughed. "You're bright, Froggy," he said, "real bright."

Eddie couldn't see what Trevor was worried about. They had found the boat washed up onshore. They couldn't find the owner because there were no registration numbers. The worst thing that could happen would be that the owner might recognize it in the paper and want it back. But after what they'd done, saving the Devin girl, maybe whoever owned it would just give it to them.

Trevor put the motor in gear and pointed the boat toward the mouth of the inlet.

"What are you doing?" Eddie said. "She might be drowning." He looked at Robbie, whose face was now as white as an empty clamshell. "She might die," he added.

The boy stared at Eddie, then shrugged his shoulders and looked at the floor of the boat. Eddie looked down, too. The toadfish by his feet was dead now, its eyes glazed, cooked by the sun.

The Devin girl couldn't have drowned, he told himself. Drowning people came up for air, they called for help. He moved his foot away from the fish, and dozens of gnats rose from its body. It was too bad they'd gotten fish blood on the floor of their new boat already, he thought. It would be hell to clean, and it would always stink.

He looked away from the fish, back to the still water. He knew he'd lost because he always lost. Trevor sat at the back of the boat. Trevor had his hand on the motor. Always.

Eddie turned around in his seat to face front. He didn't want to look at either boy any longer.

Two other boats were on their way into the harbor. The first was a Boston Whaler pulling a skier. Eddie had tried skiing only once, when the Careys made him. Each time he fell, the water forced itself into his nose. When he fell on his face, it pushed open his lids and stung his eyes. He didn't like skiing, not at all. He liked other sports, like soccer and baseball, but he came to the beach for something else. He could sit on the end of the jetty and fish by himself for hours without getting bored. He could walk among the rocks at low tide, upending them, searching for crabs, sandworms, flounder, even an occasional lobster, and never lose patience with the sea, but water skiing seemed unnatural. It was too noisy, too rough. He'd seen the Careys' oldest brother take a fall that made him tumble three or four times on the surface before he crashed into the water. A boy down the strip, Tim Landley, had even broken his leg in a fall. The water gave way when you were good to it, when you lowered your fishing line into it without asking much, or cast out to let your lure land with a *plop!*, but if you hit it hard, it hit back.

The boat swerved, and Eddie held on to the gunwale for support. He heard both Carey brothers swear. "What?" he said, turning, thinking that they'd had a change of heart, that they'd go back and check on the Devin girl after all.

"It's Rivers," Robbie said, pointing to the second boat. Rivers was the police chief. He was on his way into the harbor with his lights flashing.

"Maybe Mrs. Devin called him," Eddie said. "Maybe he's here to see about the girl."

"Would you shut up?" Trevor said. He steered the boat farther into the inlet. In a few minutes, they would round Landley Point and be out of sight. That is, if Rivers wasn't after them. If Rivers was after them, it would be a different story. They had a five-horsepower motor. The police boat motor must be at least two hundred.

The Boston Whaler was nearer now, and Eddie saw that a kid

their age was driving. The skier was a girl. She wore a black swimsuit and no ski belt. She held the towline in her mouth and was waving to the boy in the boat with both hands. The boy watched her, never looking ahead to keep on course, guiding the boat instead by instinct.

Soon the police boat was beside the Whaler, and Eddie saw Rivers yelling at the boy through a megaphone. The boy cut the motor, and the girl sank slowly into the water.

Eddie thought about Anita, rising. Then he turned to Trevor and Robbie.

"He's after *them*," he said. "They don't have a spotter."

"I know, stupid," Trevor said.

"Maybe we should go tell him about the girl," Eddie said.

The Carey boys gave him a look.

When they rounded Landley Point, they were in a small cove. The roof of the Landley house was in sight, but the rest of the house was hidden by trees. Trevor thought they should get the boat to shore and hide it in the reeds. No one else lived around there, and the Landleys kept their powerboat moored at the public beach near town and wouldn't be likely to find the clamming boat. Then they could walk or hitchhike home and return later, when the tide was up and Rivers was off duty.

About fifty yards offshore, the motor died and they couldn't restart it. There were no oars in the boat, and all three boys got out. The Carey brothers pushed from the back and Eddie pulled the rope attached to the bow. It was difficult walking through the muddy water. Sharp shells cut Eddie's feet, and when he stepped on a tuft of eelgrass, its broken blades stuck his feet like pins. Soon the water was so shallow, the boat made scraping noises as it slid along the mud, hitting bunches of mussels or an occasional rock. And soon after that, there was no water at all, just mud, and the boat became more and more difficult to move, taking on not only its own heaviness but the weight of the muck as well.

Eddie was hot now, very hot, but there was no place to get cool. The mud dried on his thighs as soon as it splashed him, and his sweat offered no relief. When it dried, its saltiness made his skin itch.

He let go of the rope, which was cutting into his skin, and grabbed the boat at the bow. He heaved when the Carey boys pushed, but it would go no farther.

"Shit," Trevor said. "We have to leave it." He looked at Robbie. "We'll come back for it later, when the tide's in," he said. "Edboy, drop the anchor."

It seemed funny, anchoring the boat now, when it was sitting on the mud, wedged between two tufts of eelgrass, but in a few hours, Eddie knew, the tide would come in and the boat would rise above the fiddler crabs, above the shellfish, above the muck, would rise on the water as his mother insisted one rose on good deeds to heaven.

He reached into the bottom of the boat to get the anchor. As he lifted it, something shiny caught his eye. Right near where his feet had been, there was a razor blade. It shot rays of sun into his eyes like someone signaling Morse code with a mirror. This message read S-T-U-P-I-D. Why hadn't he figured out why the registration numbers were missing—why, when the whole boat was newly painted, there was only one place where the paint was scraped away.

"What's going on, Frog?" Trevor said, putting the uneaten clams into the net that had held the beer cans. "Waiting for the tide to come in?"

Eddie cursed him under his breath and dropped the anchor. He watched as it settled in the mud. The claw of a fiddler crab waved at him from beneath the anchor's fluke. He wondered if he'd crushed the crab and these were just death spasms, or if it was caught. He put the heel of his foot on the crown of the anchor and pushed it further into the mud. When he lifted his foot, he could no longer see the claw, just the place where the claw had been.

The boys walked to shore through the muck, three pairs of feet making sucking noises as they lifted them to take each step, Robbie saying it sounded like farting, Trevor saying no, it sounded like something else, nudging his little brother in the ribs, Robbie snorting and laughing like he knew what the hell he was talking about.

When they reached the Careys' house, it was well after noon. They'd hiked the Landleys' private driveway, then tried to hitch along the main strip, but no one would stop except Mrs. Bowen, who leaned out her window and gave them a lecture about how they shouldn't be hitchhiking. Didn't they remember the Rowe girl, who'd been murdered, stabbed to death five years earlier by some maniac looking for hitchhikers? And by the way, did their parents know what they were doing? Then she rolled up her window, turned up the air conditioning, and drove away without them. Trevor gave her the finger as she left. One more thing Mrs. Bowen would tell Eddie's parents the next time she saw them, because Mrs. Bowen always told all the kids' parents what she'd seen their kids doing, like it was her sacred duty. Of course, her own two kids had taken off years ago, run away when they were still teenagers, and everyone knew that Mr. Bowen, who made calls from the firehouse phone booth every night after work, wasn't calling his mother.

The walk down the strip seemed endless after Mrs. Bowen left. No one talked, and when Eddie remembered the Rowe girl, he couldn't help thinking again about the Devin girl. He was sure now that she must be inside the house. Otherwise, someone would have missed her and called the police. There'd be sirens. They'd have to step off the narrow road to let the ambulance pass.

"She must be inside," Eddie said out loud.

"Who?" Trevor said. He kept walking, looking at Eddie over his shoulder.

Eddie shrugged. "You know," he said.

"Yeah, right," the boy said without anger. "Must be."

Robbie, who walked ahead, stopped walking and let his brother pass. "You really think so?" he said eagerly when Eddie reached him. When Eddie didn't answer, he added, "I do." Then he caught up with his brother and left Eddie to walk by himself.

The concrete road burned the soles of Eddie's feet and the air was hot and heavy, making it an effort to breathe. The mud that was caked on his feet dried and cracked with every step he took, and by the time he reached the Carey boys' house, it was a fine powder.

"You coming in?" Robbie said. Trevor had already started up the driveway.

"Nope," Eddie said.

Robbie started to say something, then shrugged and walked away.

On his way home, Eddie tried to walk at the edge of people's lawns in order to keep his feet from burning. There were no curbs along the strip. Most of the houses had hedges or fences along the front and only about a foot of grass between them and the road. In order to keep from stepping on the hot road, Eddie had to angle his body and stick his arms out for balance. If he stepped on a twig or a prickly weed, he jumped onto the road cursing. When he reached Anita Blake's house, he crossed the street and walked the sandy shoulder by the dunes, his back to traffic. Denny Blake was lying in the driveway under his Dodge Dart, not moving, like he was sleeping or dead, but no one else seemed to be around. Eddie crossed again when he'd passed the house, hoping Anita hadn't seen him from a window.

The driveway was empty when Eddie reached his house, and he remembered that his mother was going to be at church all day getting ready for the bazaar they had every August. He was glad not to have to face her. He was filthy and he knew he smelled of beer. She hadn't caught him drinking yet, but if she ever did, he knew that in her righteous, religious way, she'd put him through hell.

He walked around the side of the house to get to the outside shower. It usually bothered Eddie that it didn't have hot water, but today he didn't care. He looked forward to standing under its cold drizzle and finally getting some relief from the heat. The faucet was hot when he touched it, warmed by the sun. He stood under the nozzle and turned the faucet as far as he could, then jumped away yelling when the water hit him. This side of the house caught the afternoon sun, and the water in the pipes had been heated nearly to boiling. He let it run awhile, then stuck his hand under to make sure it was cold. When it was, he stepped under the nozzle and let the water rain down on him. He rubbed it into his scalp, he raised his face to it and drank it, keeping his eyes open, looking around him through the water's fluid lens at the yard, the house, the sky, and when he'd had enough, when he was shivering with the cold, he stepped once again into the steamy heat of the afternoon.

In his room, Eddie lay on his bed and thought about the morning. He realized he shouldn't have been so surprised that the boat was stolen. That was the way the Carey brothers lived. They tested every limit, or else they got bored. But Trevor never would have started the boat and left if he believed the girl had fallen in.

Eddie knew he didn't have much of a conscience, but he'd never go that far. Still, he wondered why he'd never been able to stand up to him. He'd always done what the boy told him, and where had it ever gotten him? Drunk (sometimes), in trouble (often), and today, out on the bay in a stolen boat, clamming with no license. They were lucky they hadn't been caught.

Eddie held his left hand up by the window to block the rays of sun that hit his face and made him squint. With his fingers spread wide, the extra skin looked translucent, as thin as paper. If he could spread his fingers any wider, perhaps it would tear—that was how thin it looked. Only the tiny blue blood vessels stood out in bold relief, a confusing map of city streets. Eddie had often examined the webs of skin between his fingers like this, willing them away, but it never worked. He was branded. His hand had chosen his friends, molded his personality.

He thought again about this morning, when he'd been afraid to do anything about a girl who may or may not have fallen into the water, who may or may not have drowned, who may or may not at this moment be rolling with the tide at the bottom of the bay, her white dress heavy with water, her body already a part of the muck that held so many other small deaths.

Eddie let his hand fall to the bed and rolled over on his side, his back to the window. No, he told himself. Trevor Carey had more of a conscience than that. If he'd seen her fall in, he would have stayed. Tonight the girl's mother would read her to sleep. She'd drift off slowly, her twirling on the lawn no more and no less than an exhausting, happy memory of the day.

All three boys were in the boat, shucking huge cherrystone clams and eating them. There seemed to be no end to the number of clams they could pull from the bay, each one larger than the next. Eddie worked the rake this time, and when he got it to the surface, it had a clam in it the size of a dinner plate. Trevor grabbed it and pried it open with his hands. Inside were dozens of other cherrystones the size of saucers, and they spilled into the bottom of the boat. Eddie was hot and felt slightly sick from all the clams. He stood on the bow of the boat and dove, a graceful swan dive that took him far above the water so he could see the whole strip and all its houses before he descended. As he came down, he twirled, arms spread wide, fast, then faster, until he broke the surface of the water. When he landed, the water was warm, so warm it made him sweat. He swam for a while but found no relief from the heat. He felt something splashing him and looked around. The Carey boys and the boat were far away, like a speck on the horizon, but Eddie was aware that Trevor was peeing on him. The urine left a bitter taste in his mouth, and he spit. He waited for Trevor to stop but he wouldn't. It was hitting him straight in the face, and when he turned, it landed on his head and dribbled down the front of his face so he couldn't escape it. He spit again, then took a deep breath and submerged himself. Underwater he could feel the heat of the sun more than he could see it. It seemed to be behind him, and he swam away, to the darker part of the bay, to escape it. Tufts of eelgrass and seaweed bent beneath him as he swam, as if forced by a strong wind. He was swimming toward Anita Blake, who he could see twirling naked on a long sloping lawn, smiling at him like she wanted him to come join her, but as he got closer he saw it was the Devin girl, not Anita, and he was so close he could almost touch her and when he did touch her with his ugly webbed hand he realized that it wasn't the Devin girl at all but an old rag, swirling with the current, pinned to the bottom of the bay by a barnacle-covered rock. He turned around and saw the Carey boys now and Trevor had the rake in his hand and when he pulled it out of the water there was a huge clam the size of a small child and it took the two of them to get it out of the rake and when Trevor took out his knife to cut it open Eddie saw that it wasn't a clam at all, but the Devin girl, rolled up in a ball, hugging herself to protect herself from something he couldn't see but knew was there and then he realized she was trying to protect herself from the Carey boy's knife and he yelled to let Trevor know what he was doing. He tried to swim to the surface but his foot was caught in weeds. He knew that if he struggled he'd become more entangled but struggling seemed the only thing he could do and as he did he became more entangled and struggled more and now he could hear the girl pleading, not in words, but a moan, nearly inaudible at first but then louder and louder until it was more like a scream than a moan but Eddie still could not free himself from the weeds to tell Trevor to stop cutting and then Eddie awoke to the sound of sirens.

5. Heat

When my mother offered me milk and cookies on her wedding china—which was usually reserved for Thanksgiving and Christmas—I knew something was up. It was late in the afternoon on a day that had been unbearably hot. I'd spent the day moping, as my mother would call it, sitting around the house feeling miserable, something I'd done quite a bit since that night Nita had left me by the fire. My mother poured milk into two cut crystal glasses and put out two plates of cookies. Then she invited me to come sit with her at the table.

I was having my period for the second time in my life, and my mother had decided it was time to have a talk. We'd had very few of these, the first one being after mother-daughter night when I was in fifth grade. That night, the fifth-grade girls and their mothers ate a cafeteria dinner of hamburgers and grease-soaked french fries, then sat in the All Purpose Room and watched animated films of ovaries, Fallopian tubes, and eggs. We learned how an egg was released and traveled toward the uterus. We learned how it stayed there for a while, then broke away and traveled, in a blood-red river, to an awaiting sanitary napkin. We were warned not to take baths or swim when we menstruated. We were told at what temperature to shower. We watched a film of a Betty Boop–like girl shivering when the water was too cold, sweating and wiping her Betty Boop brow when it got too hot.

That night in the All Purpose Room, we were *not* told the purpose of all those eggs and tubes and secret passageways—only that they were what made us girls, while boys had other things that made them boys. But by the time my mother sat me down for her talk three years later, I'd learned plenty from Nita, whose mother had told her in great detail about sex, whose mother had started her on tampons soon after she got her first period, and when Nita had complained about how difficult they were to insert, she had laughed and told her to imagine how much more difficult it would be to insert a penis.

To Nita, her mother was probably just what a mother was supposed to be, but to me, she seemed exotic. My mother blushed when any conversation got even slightly colorful. Nita's mother beamed, always ready with a colorful remark of her own.

Once, when she dropped by the house to pick up Nita, Mrs. Blake told my mother about a friend of hers who'd just started teaching first grade. Her friend had noticed that the class had three boys named Peter. After she took attendance, she said, "How many Peters do we have in this class?" All the little boys in the class looked down, then reluctantly raised their hands. Mrs. Blake laughed when she said this, but my mother looked dumb-founded. After a brief silence, Mrs. Blake explained that *peter* seemed to be the "in" word for little boys' penises nowadays. My mother smiled weakly, handed Nita her jacket, and hurried them out the door.

"How do you feel?" my mother said when I'd pulled in my chair.

"Okay." From where I sat at the dining-room table, I could see into the living room and out the bay window that overlooked the street, the dunes, and the beach. The water looked inviting, but I'd felt all day that a trip across the street to the beach was hardly worth it. It wouldn't be any fun without Nita. And even if it was refreshing, the relief would be only temporary. By the time I walked up the beach, up the path, across the street, over the yard, and up the stairs back into the house, I'd be just as miserable as when I started.

"Any cramps?" my mother said.

"Some."

My mother reached across the table and pushed my hair away from my face. I looked down at my cookies. They were the kind of cookies everyone in the family had always called Curly Peters—until recently. Now my mother simply called them Grandma's cookies.

"I don't know where to begin," she said. "You know I'm not good at talking about"—she stopped to search for a word—"these *things*."

"That's okay," I said, though what I really wanted to say was that I wasn't good at it either, and maybe we should just leave it at that.

I broke pieces from a cookie and nibbled at them. My mother ran her fingernails across the cut crystal of her milk glass.

"How much do you already know?" she said after a while. "I mean, you being friends with Anita Blake and all." She paused.

"I mean, she's very well—" She started over. "Her mother's always been—" She tried again. "She probably knows quite a bit."

"Some," I said. "Enough." I pulled my chair closer to the table, then pushed it back. "I guess," I added.

I was thinking about what Nita had said about me doing it with Eddie Barnicle that time I was worried about the jellyfish. I looked up at my mother. "When can you do it?" I asked. "I mean, is there a time when it's okay and a time when it's not?"

"You can do it when you're married," my mother said, placing her glass on the table with a dull thud.

"Oh," I said. I looked at the tablecloth, at the place where some milk had splashed, and noticed the scallop shells woven into the linen. I finished my cookies and took a sip of milk. This wasn't the answer I'd wanted. I knew it was possible to do it before you were married, before you were sixteen, even. What I really wanted to know was what that stuff I'd thought was jellyfish was for.

My mother started running her fingernails over her glass again. "You probably want to know how it's done," she said, sounding distressed. She looked down and took a deep breath, as if she were about to go under. "When two people love each other," she said, speaking very quickly, her words tumbling over each other, "the-man-gets-hard-and-dry-and-the-woman-gets-soft-and-wet." Her face was flushed and she was breathing heavily when she finished, as if she had just come up for air. I waited for her to say more, but I soon realized she had no more to say.

Now, from what Nita had told me, I thought I knew at least a little about the mechanics of sex. But if I had been on the verge of something—on the verge of figuring it all out, maybe—I was completely lost now. I had no idea what my mother meant. *Hard and dry* might be an apt description of my father in one of his rare angry moments. *Soft and wet* might well describe my mother the few times I'd seen her cry. What it all had to do with love was a mystery to me.

"Well," she said after an awkward silence. She stood up and pushed her chair in. "How about a walk on the beach?" She left the room and started down the stairs to the door without waiting for an answer, and I followed. The heat hit us both with a blast when my mother opened the door, but I knew neither one of us wanted to go back inside. In spite of the attic fan, things were much hotter in there.

When we reached the end of the driveway, I noticed Trevor and Robbie Carey down a ways. They were taking turns pushing each other into the street. Eddie Barnicle wasn't with them, which was unusual. Nita said Eddie clung to Trevor Carey like a barnacle to a rock. The only difference between Trevor and a rock, Nita said, was that a rock had more intelligence. The only difference between Eddie and a *real* barnacle, she said, was that a barnacle would hurt you if you stepped on it.

Nita always thought this last part was hilarious, but I never laughed. Maybe Eddie needed the Carey brothers the same way I needed Nita, I thought. Maybe they made him feel like he mattered.

Although it was still hot, it was late enough so that most families who'd spent the day on the beach were packing up and heading home. We turned toward the Neck and walked just above the high-tide mark, a few yards from the water. We both kept our heads down out of habit, looking for scallop shells, jingle shells, or lady slippers among the hundreds of mussel shells that seemed to be overtaking the beach. We looked up when two high school boys jogged by, bare-chested and glistening with sweat.

"I suppose you and Anita will be going to parties with boys

soon," my mother said after a moment. She sounded sad. She leaned over to pick up a jingle shell, then handed it to me. "Won't you?"

"I guess," I said. I didn't remind my mother that I'd already been to parties with boys and had decided that parties with only girls were much more fun. We'd turn up the music, turn out the lights, and practice dancing. Then we'd turn on the lights, and the braver girls—girls like Nita—would keep on dancing, swinging their hips and shimmying, while the rest of us watched in awe. When boys were at a party, no one ever danced, no matter how loud the music was.

"When I was your age," my mother said, "we didn't have to worry about things like—" She sighed. "We didn't have to worry about boys. Things were much easier."

I kept walking in silence. My mother was teary-eyed. *Getting soft and wet on me*, I thought.

"You're growing so fast," my mother said. "I used to think we could have this talk when you were older, but things have changed."

My mother took my hand and stopped, so that I had to stop, too. "Promise me," she said, squeezing my hand, "promise me you'll wait until—at least until you're older."

I nodded, not sure what *older* meant. After all, I'd be older tomorrow. I'd be older in an hour. But it didn't really matter what my mother meant, because I figured I'd be ancient—twenty-five or thirty, even—before I was able to figure it all out.

We were almost to the jetty before my mother spoke again. "You and Anita haven't seen each other in a while, have you?" she said.

"No," I said. "She's busy, I guess." I walked a little faster, around a gray rowboat that was pulled up onshore beside the jetty.

I smelled something foul nearby, and when I looked into the boat, I saw a dead oyster crusher under the middle seat. It was covered with gnats and had sunken eyes. The sight and the smell of it turned my stomach. Nita would laugh, but this was just the kind of discovery that could keep me from swimming at night for the rest of my life.

"Nita's mother needs her right now," I said when we'd passed the boat. "To do things."

My mother stopped and touched my shoulder. She started to say something, then cleared her throat instead.

I pulled away and climbed up the jetty, then jumped onto the sand on the other side. I didn't want to talk about Nita. I didn't know *how* to talk about Nita without telling my mother about Mrs. Blake.

"You're Anita's best friend," my mother said when she reached me. "Aren't you?"

"I don't know," I said. "I guess so."

"You tell her she can come to our house anytime she wants, okay?"

I looked up at my mother, and that was when I knew that she knew.

We walked in silence almost all the way to the Coast Guard station. Then my mother started to talk, and any chance we might have had to talk about Anita and Mrs. Blake was washed away in the flood tide of her words. She talked about all the things she usually talked about, and what she usually talked about was not momentous, not deep, not personal. First she talked about school, about the courses she knew I would be taking. Then she talked about Mrs. Bowen, "that poor woman," though everyone else in town seemed to think she was a nut. She went on and on, and soon I stopped listening, thinking instead about the kind of talk

Nita would have with her mother if they walked on the beach like this. Mrs. Blake could talk about love. Mrs. Blake could talk about sex. Mrs. Blake could even talk about her own death. My mother's talk was all small talk, because, I concluded, the life she shared with me and my father was so dull, so insignificant, so incredibly small.

At the point right before the lighthouse, we stopped. The heat was still intense, and my T-shirt and shorts stuck to me. I pulled my shirt away from my body and blew into it. My mother took off her loafers and walked up to her knees in the water. She splashed her face and arms.

"You'd better cool down some, too," she said. "I don't want you getting heat stroke."

I resented being told what to do, but I was hot. When I stepped into the water, I nearly tripped over a pair of horseshoe crabs, mating in the surf. The smaller male was on the back of the female, and they were heading toward the sandy shore, where the female would lay her eggs. I remembered that when we were younger, Nita and I had picked the mating couples up and pulled them apart, as if it were a game. Just thinking about it embarrassed me now. I looked up at my mother, hoping she hadn't seen them.

She was looking up the beach toward the lighthouse. I looked, too. There must have been a dozen horseshoe crabs mating in the shallows.

"Oh, dear," my mother said uncomfortably.

"But it's *August*," I said. As a rule, I knew that horseshoe crabs mated in May—June at the latest. Though they'd been getting it right for millions of years, perhaps we'd finally figured out a way to confound them—maybe it was the thermal pollution at the power plant that had done it, or maybe it was Mother Nature, rushing in where my own mother feared to tread.

"Isn't that appropriate?" my mother said. She looked down at the two crabs mating at our feet. "It's unavoidable, isn't it? It's as if someone planned this—like one of your father's practical jokes." She sighed. "What I told you about the man and the woman," she said, "that's what *my* mother told *me*." She smiled. "It doesn't make any sense at all, does it?"

I looked up at her, then back to the two crabs. "They both look pretty wet to me," I said.

"Oh, dear," my mother said again. She smiled. Then she giggled like a young girl. Then she laughed out loud for a long time, and the longer she laughed, the younger she seemed. After a while she fell to her knees, still laughing. I sat on the sand next to her and joined in, not exactly sure why.

When we could both breathe again, my mother got up and started to run. "Catch me if you can," she called to me. I ran after her, trying to keep my feet in her footprints, but after a while she ran too close to the waves, and they washed the new footprints away before I could reach them.

She stopped at the jetty, and when I caught up, she hugged me.

"Don't worry," she said. "You'll figure it out when the time comes." She held me at arm's length, and I looked into her face. Her eyes were as gray as the Sound on a cloudy day, and much deeper. She pulled me close again. "And you'll enjoy it, too, you know. That's the beauty of it."

I smelled the saltiness of her sweat and felt her tears streaming down my shoulder. Maybe my mother wasn't so ordinary, I thought. She was young, she was happy with her life, and at this moment, she was incredibly alive.

"Don't ever die," I whispered, putting my arms around her. My mother held me tighter, and I took this as her promise.

6. Sirens

If any of the evening commuters on their way out to the Neck thought there was anything strange about the sight, they didn't stop to say so.

And what a sight it must be, Nita thought. There was Mrs. Blake, the high school home economics teacher, thinner than she'd ever been, perhaps as a result of one of those supermarket-checkout-counter-fad-diets—beer and grapefruit, maybe—already in her bathrobe (or perhaps it was *still* in her bathrobe) at seven o'clock at night, hair unkempt (that would be Mrs. Bowen's word), leaning on her poor daughter, drunk as Dean Martin. Her daughter, poor girl, was probably taking her out on the beach to dunk her, sober her up some before poor Mr. Blake returned home. It was a disgraceful sight for a schoolteacher, and they hoped none of the children had seen. They'd go to the school board in the fall to discuss the matter. *We said so a million times, but you wouldn't listen. Give a teacher the summer off and look what happens.*

． ． ．

"Your father had to go in early today," Nita's mother had said from the top of the stairs that morning.

"I'll fix breakfast," Nita said, hoping her mother wouldn't notice her wet hair. "Why don't you come down?" She started toward the kitchen.

"I can't," her mother said.

Nita stopped.

"I've been standing here since your father left, looking down the stairs." She leaned heavily against the wall. "I called you, but you didn't answer, and I guess Denny couldn't hear me from his room. I was worried, but I couldn't find the energy to look for you." She started to cry. "I couldn't find the energy to move."

Nita climbed the stairs and put her arm around her mother's waist. "Hold on to me," she said. "We'll go down together."

Her mother put her hand on Nita's shoulder, leaning heavily, and Nita pulled her close. She smelled nice, like morning, but underneath the familiar scent was something sour, a scent Nita had never noticed before, and it alarmed her. They took one step at a time, resting after every two or three. It seemed it would take forever to get to the bottom. When they finally did, Nita's mother collapsed in a chair near the staircase. "I'd like to sit out back," she said, holding her hand to her heart as if she'd had the wind knocked out of her. "Just give me a moment." She leaned back and closed her eyes.

Getting her mother settled on the back porch was difficult. She'd never been this bad before, had always, except for that brief time after a hospital stay in July, been able to get around on her own. Now she held on to the picnic table for support while Nita adjusted the lounge chair and put it in the shade of a tree. It was already unbearably hot, and Nita knew it would only get worse.

But her mother asked her to move the chair into the sun. She was cold, she said. There was already a touch of fall in the air; she could feel it. Nita did as she was told and got her mother a blanket when she asked for one. She couldn't believe it. It was ninety degrees outside, and her mother was freezing to death.

When Nita returned a while later to put sunscreen on her mother's face, her mother's eyes were closed. She opened them when she heard her daughter sit beside her. "Anita, honey," she said, reaching for Nita's hand and holding it. "Could you bring me a shell? I'd like to hold one. I'd like to look at one. I haven't been to the beach in so long. I was just trying to remember what it's like."

"It's right across the street, Mom," Nita said. "You could look out the front window. I could take you there."

"It wouldn't be the same," Nita's mother said. "I'd like to remember it the way it was before."

Before what? Nita wondered. The power plant? The oil spills? The popularity of powerboats? "Before what?" she asked.

"Before everything changed," her mother said, and closed her eyes again. "Before this long, cold summer."

Nita went into the house and picked up the first shells she saw—a pair of cherrystone clamshells sitting on the coffee table in the living room. She started back to her mother, then reconsidered. Instead, she went into the bathroom and got a towel. Then she went from room to room, gathering shells like wildflowers. By the time she returned to her mother, she had collected all the shells in the house. She put the towel on her mother's lap and opened it.

Her mother smiled at her. "That's wonderful, Anita," she said. She picked up two handfuls and dropped the shells through her fingers like coins. "You've brought me the whole beach." She held the pair of cherrystone clamshells and rubbed her thumb along the inside of one of them. She pointed out the purple part to Nita, as she'd done when Nita was a child. "This is wampum," she said. "You used to be able to buy anything with this. Anything at all." She closed her eyes and continued to rub the shell.

Nita left her mother alone for most of the day, tending to her only when she needed to go to the bathroom, and then later when she needed lunch—a tremendous word, considering what her mother actually ate. Her mother thought she should call Molly, should go to the beach and enjoy herself like other girls her age. What her mother had forgotten was that most other girls her age didn't enjoy themselves at all. They worried about liking boys, or like Nita, they wondered why they didn't; they waited impatiently for their first period, and suffered when it finally came. So Nita spent the day watching soap operas, those pathetic little tragedies squeezed between advertisements for laundry detergent, disposable douche, and feminine wash. The biggest tragedy on television, Nita thought, was that women were expected to worry about things like cleaning their husbands' shirt collars and washing their kitchen floors, about painting their lips the lushest shade of red, smelling just right for their men. As far as she could see, there wasn't much to look forward to.

Nita went to the beach for another swim late in the afternoon. The little girls next door were using their dragnet. As they pulled it deeper into the water, it filled and expanded, like a sheet in the breeze. Then one of them stopped while the other turned widely toward shore. When the net was parallel to the shoreline, they both ran it in. It began to collapse in the shallow water and fell completely in on itself when they dragged it up onshore, but when they spread it out, Nita saw the silver slapping of shiners and killys on the damp sand.

There were clusters of women and children all the way down the strip of beach. It was so hot that no one sat on the multicolored towels scattered on the sand like the petals of some huge flower. Instead, the children played in the water while the mothers stood knee-deep, watching. Nita could hear their screams of laughter, could see the bright colors of their floats and beach balls. One child ran out of the water, and his mother greeted him with a towel. She tousled his hair with it, then wrapped it around his body. She rubbed him all over with it, and he squirmed, trying to get away from her. Nita remembered how reassuring it was, having someone there to dry you off. She remembered running out of the early June water or climbing out of a hot bath in the winter and having no time at all to be cold, because her mother or grandmother was always there with a towel, ready to give her a rubdown. When she was five, her grandmother gave her a pale blue towel with a hood on it. It had eyelets with a shoelace running through them so she could tie it under her chin, and the towel was so big, it trailed around her ankles. But now her grandmother was dead and the towel was a rag her mother used to dust the furniture.

Nita looked toward the water again, where teenage boys drove powerboats wildly and teenage girls drove teenage boys wild. The oldest Carey boy drove by in his boat while his girlfriend lounged on the deck in a string bikini. Two of the other Carey boys, the ones near Nita's age, sat in a gray wooden boat anchored near the jetty and watched their brother. When he drove by with his girlfriend, they hooted and whistled, and the girlfriend acknowledged them by tossing her head and letting her hair stream behind her in a breeze whose only source was driving nowhere fast in a motorboat on a hot summer day.

When Nita walked into the water, she felt the Carey boys' eyes on her. Of course they were remembering this morning.

They were probably making disgusting comments, though that would be nothing new. They were probably drooling, and that wasn't new, either. They were a strange bunch, the entire crew of them. She didn't know a lot about them, but what she did know was this: They didn't have a mother, hadn't had a mother for as long as anyone could remember. No one had even seen a woman dropping by the house. Mrs. Bowen insisted she remembered a series of boy toddlers and even infants, but no one could remember a Mrs. Carey. Some people had suggested she was kept locked inside the house. Other people had suggested there never was one. Molly's mother—who could never think ill of anyone—probably thought that each boy in turn just appeared on the doorstep, and Mr. Carey—who everyone in town believed was a nice person —took them in and treated them like his own sons. Of course, quite a few of them looked an awful lot alike, but Molly's mother probably thought that was some sort of bizarre coincidence.

Nita herself was in favor of the theory she and Molly had developed: One day all the Carey boys had crawled out from under a big ugly rock.

She took one last look at the boys, blinking and sunning themselves on the boat, and dove in. She swam straight out, as fast as she could. She could hear the powerboats nearby. If the drivers didn't see her, they could hit her, chop her up in the blades of their motors. There'd be blood and later, maybe even sharks. Women would call their children out of the water or go in and grab them, dragging them screaming to shore. Boys in boats twice as large as any shark would make excuses to their girlfriends to go back to the boat ramp. Yes, Nita thought, if she got hit by a motorboat, she could clear this place out pretty quick.

She remembered the time she really had attracted a shark to shore. She was ten and was playing on the sandbar, doing handstands in the water, then somersaults, always touching down again, digging her feet into the cool fine sand. Her mother was in the aluminum rowboat with Denny, fishing out past the Big Rock. Nita had just come up from a series of backward somersaults when she heard her mother yelling and motioning for her to go to shore. She wouldn't. She was old enough to swim alone. Denny had been swimming alone when he was nine. She went under for a handstand. When she came up again, other women on the beach were waving to her and yelling, too. When she looked toward the rowboat she saw it: a fin. Denny was sitting on the floor of the boat looking terrified, and her mother was standing in the center with an oar raised above her head.

Getting to shore was the scariest thing she'd ever done. Swimming wasn't fast enough, and the thought of a shark grabbing her by her kicking feet terrified her. Running in the chest-deep water was like running in a nightmare. No matter how hard she tried, she got nowhere. Then, when she still seemed miles from shore, a woman from one of the summer rentals—Nita remembered her as huge and powerful—lifted her up and in one great swing deposited her on the sand. She knelt down and patted Nita on the cheek, then disappeared into the crowd that had gathered on the beach. By the end of the summer, Nita began to believe that the woman was a dream she'd had, because though she looked for her all summer, she never saw her again.

When her mother and Denny got to shore, they explained that they'd caught a large blackfish and had trouble getting the hook out. There had been a lot of blood. They left the fish hanging out of the back of the boat while they tried for more. That was what had attracted the shark, Nita's mother said. But Nita knew it was something else that had put her mother in danger. She was having her first period, and her mother had given her a huge sanitary napkin that was uncomfortable and bulged in the bottom of her bathing suit like a diaper. In a pamphlet she got from the school nurse, it had said that girls should never go swimming when they menstruated. They should sit on the beach and wait it out. In the pamphlet they'd never explained why, but that day, Nita knew. It was to keep you from attracting sharks.

Nita filled her lungs with air and went under. She imagined drowning in the middle of all this activity. She'd go under three times, as someone had told her drowning people did. Each time up she'd wave, and the people onshore would wave back. Each time down she'd pull in a little more water. Then later, when the farewells were long over, her body would wash up onshore, abandoned and beautiful.

Because it wouldn't be *her* washing up onshore, it would be her body. That was the way people talked about dead people. Not "Anita Blake washed up onshore," but "The body of Anita Blake washed up onshore." When her grandmother had died, the people at the hospital had asked her mother what they should do with "the body." They did it all the time. "The body of a man was found in the Dumpster." "A woman's body was found in the trunk of the car." They always talked as if once you found a woman's body, you might actually be able to find, as well, the woman who owned it.

Nita touched bottom with her feet, but it wasn't the same. The powerboats filled the water with a tinny sound, like the buzz of huge mosquitoes. She heard rocks being hit together, sand crunching. With people around, the water was a hostile, noisy place. She let her breath out and shot to the surface. She'd come back to swim later, when the beach was empty.

When Nita got to the back porch, her mother was still lying in the lounge chair. There was a pile of shells on the floor next to her and another pile in her lap. She had a pair of shells in her hands, and as Nita approached she snapped them apart, throwing one on the floor and dropping the other in her lap. She had already broken nearly every pair in two.

"I've been making plans," she said when she saw her daughter.

Nita and her mother stood at the end of the driveway, waiting for a break in traffic. She had waited to take her mother across until the police cars had passed, but now she heard more sirens. Her mother leaned into her ear to speak. "They're not for me, are they?"

Nita shook her head, but worried just the same. Maybe one of the commuters *had* noticed them, maybe one of them had called. When the traffic broke, Nita could see the flashing lights of an ambulance approaching from the Neck. She pulled her mother across the street, hoping not to be seen. When they reached the path in the beach grass, her mother stumbled and fell. Nita tried to pull her up, but she had rolled into a fetal position. She lay on her side, with the grass all around her.

"Get up, Mom," Nita said. "Let me help you."

But Nita's mother made no effort to move. She just lay there and said, "The grass is so high, I could hide in here for weeks and they'd never find me."

"Who?" Nita said.

Nita's mother looked up at her. "You know," she said. Then she closed her eyes.

The ambulance sped by, then another police car. Nita crouched by her mother in the grass and watched them go. When they had passed, she struggled to get her to her feet. When she did, she could see her mother's form in the matted-down beach grass. But even as she watched, blades of grass were popping back up. It wouldn't be long before it was impossible to tell exactly where she had fallen. Anyone else wouldn't be able to tell that her mother had been there at all.

"Our swim, Mom," she said as she pulled her to her feet and hoisted her arm around her shoulder.

"That's right," her mother said. She squeezed Nita's shoulder gently and whispered, "You were going to take me to the water."

As they made their way toward the water, Nita's mother seemed to weaken. It was more and more difficult for Nita to keep her balance as they walked, her mother's arm slung heavily over her shoulder, and when they were a few yards from the water's edge, Nita was forced to carry her. It was a struggle to lift her, and when she held her in her arms, she had to stand still a moment to get her balance. Beneath her mother's thin cotton robe Nita could feel the sharp blades of her shoulders, the bones of her legs. The robe was open slightly at the top and Nita could see part of her mother's breast. It seemed to be all skin now, no firmness, just an empty sack of skin. Where was there room for any life in her mother's body? Where did her mother keep herself?

Nita trudged to the water. Her mother was much heavier than she looked, but as the water rose around them, Nita's load lightened. When she was chest deep she still held her arms out in front of her, under her mother, but only to keep her from drifting away or sinking. A chill gripped her mother's body, shaking her uncontrollably, but before Nita could do anything, the chill passed.

Her mother took her arms from around Nita's neck and dropped her head back to wet her hair. It floated around her face, framed it. "This is wonderful, Anita," she said, sighing deeply. "My body. It's as if it's no longer there."

Nita looked at her mother and smiled. This was what she'd hoped for. She'd show her mother how good the water could make you feel, how it could make you forget everything but the time spent suspended, the time when nothing but the moment mattered.

Nita sank into the water and put her arm across her mother's chest. Then she swam on her side, her mother in tow, until it was too deep for either of them to stand. When Nita stopped to rest, her mother pulled away.

"I don't know why I let you do that," she said. She was treading water now, facing her daughter. "I could have swum out by myself, but it was so nice, floating along like that." She smiled. "I haven't felt like that in ages."

"You're not tired?" Nita said.

Her mother shook her head. "I could stay out here forever. If they'd let me," she added. "It's beautiful."

"It's nice underwater, too," Nita said, remembering the morning. "Another world."

"Let's see it then," her mother said. "We'll go down together."

Nita hesitated. "I don't think you're well enough," she said. "You can hardly walk."

"I feel fine," her mother answered. "Would I be out here at all if I didn't feel fine?"

"You didn't seem fine a little while ago." Nita could feel the tears in her eyes, and she splashed her face with water to keep her mother from seeing them.

Her mother smiled. "We're all dying, Anita," she said simply. "I'm just going about it more efficiently than most people." She splashed more water in Nita's direction. "But we're not out here to talk about that, are we?" she said. "We're not out here to be sad."

Her mother took a deep breath and went under. Nita followed, but her mother sank much more quickly than she did, and it was a struggle for Nita to keep up with her. When they were both near the bottom, Nita's mother put her arms around her and held on. Nita wanted to hug her back, but if she stopped moving her hands, she was afraid they'd both float to the surface.

Her mother nestled her head on Nita's shoulder. Her body

floated parallel to the bottom and her hair floated above her, tick-ling Nita's face. Nita struggled to keep her breath in, but her mother seemed to make no effort at all. If her arms weren't wrapped so snugly around Nita's neck, Nita might have thought she was asleep.

Only a few seconds had passed when Nita began to panic. Her lungs were ready to explode, but her mother showed no sign of discomfort, no sign that she wanted to return to the surface at all. The only signs that she was even alive were the occasional bubbles escaping from her nostrils. And she still held her daughter around the neck.

Nita tapped her mother repeatedly on the shoulder. She tried to pull her arms from around her neck, but her mother wouldn't release her.

And then Nita was afraid that she'd killed her, that her mother had drowned hanging on to her, that the air escaping through her nostrils now and then was the breath of life, leaving her, and that they'd have to pry her stiffened arms from around Nita's neck in order to bury her—or worse, that Nita would die too, and she'd never be able to explain to her father and Denny why she'd taken her mother to the water.

She had to act quickly. She made herself sink so that her feet touched bottom and her knees bent beneath her, and then she pushed off, climbing the deep water as she'd climb a rope, feeling the pain of ascending in her arms and in her lungs. Her mother's arms were still wrapped tightly around her when she broke the surface. Nita coughed and gagged as she recovered her breath, shaking her mother by the shoulders as she did. Her mother's eyes were closed, but Nita could see her chest expanding and con-tracting, expanding and contracting. Her breaths were long and deep, yet seemed to take little effort. In a moment her mother opened her eyes and let go of her.

"You were right," she said. "It's another world."

"We almost drowned down there," Nita said. She was surprised when her voice came out a yell. She tried to calm down, but began to cry instead. "And you wouldn't have cared, would you?" She was crying so hard it was difficult to keep her head above water. "You don't want to live. You're killing yourself."

"Of course I care, Anita," her mother said. She treaded water calmly at her daughter's side. "I just wasn't ready to come up." She splashed water playfully in Nita's face. "That's typical of me, isn't it? I'm not ready for most things."

Nita's mother swam to shore on her own. She did the side-stroke, pulling and pushing the water with her hands and doing a scissor kick that sent her gracefully across the water. Just as her body began to sink, she'd start the stroke over again and recover her buoyancy. As she swam, she seemed strong and steady, not at all like she was on land when she tried to walk or to lift herself from a chair. Nita swam beside her, adopting her rhythm, breathing the way she did. It was calming, not having to think about swimming, mimicking instead the motions of her mother.

When they reached the shore, Nita tried to help her mother out of the water, but she pulled away and walked up the beach on her own. Her progress was slow. She'd lost the grace she had in the water, but Nita was glad anyway, because it was progress.

When she was a child, her brother Denny had tried to teach her about regeneration. He'd pulled the claw off a crab and Nita was mad at him, but he swore it would grow back. He showed her starfish in all stages—the stumps of one or two or three of their arms promising new growth. He showed her large crabs with tiny new claws where the old ones had been. But Nita hadn't believed him. It didn't seem possible to her that a crab or a starfish could grow something from nothing. It didn't seem possible that there could be regeneration at all. But now, watching her mother's progress up the beach, she began to believe. They'd do this again tomorrow, and the next day and the next. If they kept it up, she didn't see why her mother couldn't be perfectly well by the time school started.

Mrs. Blake collapsed before she reached the path. She folded up, fell in on herself like a net pulled from the water.

Nita ran to her. Then she sat, her mother's head cradled in her lap, and waited until her mother was ready to go home.

7. Cicadas

the dampness from Eddie's shorts had soaked into the bed-
clothes. It was a warm dampness that turned cold when he moved
away from it. It reminded him of all the times he'd wet his bed as a
child. The feeling he had on waking was the same, too—the feeling that he'd done something terribly wrong, and that nothing he
could do now could undo it. He sat up and swung his feet to the
ground, anxious to find his land legs. His mouth was dry and
cottony, stale with the taste of beer and clams. He realized that
was all he'd eaten all day, beer and clams, and it was nearly seven
o'clock. He couldn't believe he'd slept so long. His fatigue was like
a strong current, pulling him out, out. He'd fought it as long as he
could, and then he'd given himself up, as a drowning person gives
himself up to the sea. It was the sirens that had saved him, pulled
him back to shore. He wondered if they were real. Was that them
in the distance, toward town, or were they stuck somewhere in the

back of his mind? It didn't matter, he decided. Real or not, it was way too late for them to be for the Devin girl. Someone was having a heart attack; someone was having a baby.

When Eddie reached the top of his driveway, he was already sweating. Without the strong midday sun, his sweat didn't dry. It made his clothing stick to him. It dribbled down his legs like warm pee. He ran down the hill toward the beach, creating his own breeze. It felt cool on his damp body, and he spread his arms wide as he ran so that the air hit him all over. He started walking again at the beginning of the strip. He was hot again. He was thirsty. But he felt good. He would walk on the beach. He would end his day the way he began it. He'd balance things. A terrible thing had almost happened today, and then it hadn't. A walk on the beach would end the day right.

The sun was setting on the bay side when Eddie reached the dunes. He had already scrambled halfway up one of them when a car slowed on its way from the Neck. It stopped, and Mrs. Bowen leaned out the window. Her hair had curler marks in it, as if she'd removed the curlers and then forgotten to brush it. Her eye makeup was smeared. She ran her hand under her nose before she talked to him. Maybe she drove by the firehouse and saw her husband in the phone booth, Eddie thought. Maybe after all this time, she's figured things out.

"Edwin Barnicle," she said. "What are you doing out at this hour?"

"Going for a walk on the beach," Eddie said, thinking, My name is Edward, not Edwin, then wondering why she cared, and then remembering that she cared about everyone's business but her own. He guessed she hadn't seen her husband.

"Do your parents know?" she asked.

"Yeah," Eddie said. "They told me I could go as long as I'm

back by—" He hesitated, not sure what time it was now. "Nine," he said.

"Well," Mrs. Bowen began. She undid her seat belt so she could lean farther out the window, and Eddie prepared himself for one of her longer speeches. "I'm surprised that *any* parents *any*-where would let a child out so late—and right near the water, too, after what happened today. Some people have absolutely no"—she hesitated, searching for a word, and as she did Eddie felt a sickness start in his stomach—"prudence," she said, spitting the *p* from her lips like a stripped fruit pit. "Prudence," she said again, as if she liked the shape of the word in her mouth. "You know, after what happened to the Devin girl today." Eddie slid down the dune. "Poor thing. And all because her mother was too—too *busy*," she said with disgust, "to realize the poor child had gotten up and headed outside," she said. "As if anything were more important than that poor little child." She looked into Eddie's face. "Why, what's the matter?" she said. "I'm only looking out for you. God knows, no one else seems to—I mean after I saw you walking with those *awful* Carey boys this afternoon, and you with such nice, decent parents. It's beyond me. Really, it's beyond me."

"What happened to her?" Eddie said, his voice cracking.

"What?" Mrs. Bowen said. "Speak up, Edwin, or come closer. How can you expect me to hear you when you're standing there on the other side of the street and I've got the car running?"

Eddie slid the rest of the way down the dune to the sandy shoulder. "What happened to her?" he repeated.

"Why, she drowned, Edwin," Mrs. Bowen said, as if this were only logical. She turned off her car without pulling to the side of the road. "Or her mother drowned her by ignoring her. Same difference. But it's too terrible. I hate to talk about it. Hate to even think about it." A car came from behind and honked, but Mrs. Bowen ignored it. Its driver glared at her as he pulled around her.

When the car was out of sight, Mrs. Bowen continued. "It reminds me of the Rowe girl. Oh, God, how awful." She stared into Eddie's eyes to make sure she still had his attention. "The Devin child jumped off the dock," she continued, relishing the attention he gave her, "or maybe wandered into the water, right into the mud and the eelgrass, then got tangled in that like—" She rubbed at her eyes and sniffled. "Terrible," she said. "They had to cut her out. When they finally got her poor body up, it was wrapped in grass. Mr. Covelli next door said he even saw eelgrass wrapped around her neck—too awful to even think about.

"They spent all day looking for her, all around the neighborhood. Can you believe it? No one even thought to look in the water—and with the water right in her own backyard. Can you believe no one even thought to look there? Of course, that would have been my first thought, but I'm not the poor girl's mother, thank God. Wouldn't you think to look in the water first thing? Well?" she said, and then continued.

"Blue in the face, is what I heard." She settled herself once more in her seat. "Well, look at me, and just out for a trip to the Dairy Barn before Mr. Bowen gets home." And then she pulled away without turning on her lights, went right down the strip with her lights out.

The light had drained from the sky, but the sand beneath Eddie's feet glowed, as if it remembered the day. He walked to the water and sat down. He noticed three dried stalks of eelgrass next to him, sticking out of the sand as if someone had placed them there for a purpose. He pulled them out of the sand and broke them into small pieces, then scattered the pieces on the water. Some of them blew across the water's surface and flew away, some took on its heaviness and were pulled under by the next wave. Eddie put his toes at the edge of the wet sand. He looked out over the water, hoping that Anita Blake would appear between him and the horizon, would let him start the day again, but he knew it was too late, too dark. He started to draw her shape in the sand with his finger. A wave came up higher than all the others and filled what Eddie had drawn as her head. The water soaked into the sand, leaving only foam.

He stared at the place the wave had been. He pictured the Devin girl the way Mrs. Bowen had described her. He remembered her in his dream. It was his fault, he was sure of it. It was his fault for not being someone else.

"If I'd have sat at the stern and run the motor, we could have saved her," he said aloud. The sound of his voice surprised him, and he looked around to make sure no one was near. "I would have," he said, a little louder this time.

But no one heard because no one was there to hear.

Eddie found the clamming boat pulled up on the beach on the other side of the jetty. That meant that the Careys had gone back to the Landleys' when the tide came in. He wondered if they knew about the Devin girl. He doubted it. They would have gone for the boat hours before he'd heard the siren. Besides, if they had smelled trouble, they would have stayed away. And Mrs. Bowen would never stop to tell them. No one would.

He climbed into the boat and sat at the bow, where he'd sat this morning. The rake was balanced, prongs up, on the other two seats. Eddie watched the moon rising over the Sound and wished he were far away, looking at this same moon from some other place. Some of the rocks on the jetty were covered with mica, and it sparkled in the moonlight. The white rock, the one he'd been drawn to in the summers as a child because it was cooler than all the others, even when the sun was unbearable, glowed like something from another planet.

He tried to think of what he could have done differently. Say he'd never gone clamming at all. Say he'd stayed on the beach and talked to Anita Blake. But that wouldn't have worked. She'd never talked to him before, and she wasn't exactly dressed for conversation when he saw her. And besides, the Devin girl still would have fallen in, and the Careys still would have left—only he wouldn't have been there to know about it.

Would that have been better?

He guessed so.

Or say he'd fought with Trevor when he wouldn't turn back. He would have lost, of course, with two against one. But say he'd gotten Robbie on his side, or say Rivers had seen them fighting and come by to see what the trouble was. Then he could have told Rivers, and Rivers would have been so concerned about finding the Devin girl, he would have sped away without noticing the beer cans, without noticing the dozens of clams in the bottom of the boat. Besides, how much trouble could that be?

Yes, Eddie thought, he could have done something differently.

He stomped his foot in anger on the bottom of the boat and felt something stick it. He lifted his foot and examined his sole. He'd kicked the razor blade, and it had cut cleanly into the ball of his foot where it stayed, glinting up at him. He was surprised that he felt no pain. When he pulled it out, he realized that the cut was shallow, but clean.

Then it began to hurt. He dropped the blade to the bottom of the boat and put his chin in his hand. He watched his foot bleed, watched the way the slit filled up with his blood before it spilled over and dripped down his sole to the floor. Then he looked at the floor. The razor blade caught the light from the moon, and Eddie remembered that about the day, too—remembered the way he'd figured out the boat was stolen. If someone came upon him now as he sat here, he'd probably be arrested. He deserved it, though, he thought. They all three deserved it.

Eddie picked up the blade again and knelt down facing the back of the boat. He could have been praying, he thought. He could have been praying for the soul of the Devin girl, though he didn't believe in souls, didn't believe in prayers, either. If prayers worked, his hand would have been fixed a long time ago. If prayers worked, his parents would have taken him to a doctor as he'd asked, and let the doctor cut away the flesh between his fingers. But prayers didn't work. His mother had seemed shocked at the idea that he'd want to change anything. When he asked, she took his hand in hers and kissed each web. We can't change what God has made, she said, and that was the end of that.

Well, it was time to try.

He put his left hand on the rowing seat, the seat that Robbie Carey had sat in this morning, and spread his fingers wide. He held the blade above them. If he was going to change things, he'd start right now.

He pushed the blade quickly into the web of skin between his pinkie and ring finger.

It hurt. It hurt like he hadn't imagined it could hurt, but he kept pushing until he felt the blade dig into the thick coat of paint on the seat. He kept his mouth closed, his lips tightly pursed as he cut. His eyes and nose filled quickly with water, and soon he had to open his mouth to breathe.

He slid the blade back and forth in the groove he'd dug in the paint, to make sure he cut away all the skin. He bit his lower lip as he did this last part, trying to create some other pain, one that was more familiar. Then he started on the other web. When he cut into the skin this time, he let out a sharp cry.

"He's here," a voice said from somewhere in the shadows in front of him.

Eddie lifted the blade and looked up, frightened.

Trevor stood at the stern of the boat. He put one foot up on it, then put his elbow on his raised knee, his chin in his hand. His upturned face was lit by the moon, but the rest of him was in darkness. Robbie stood behind him. He didn't speak. His shoulders slumped, and from the way the younger boy stood, Eddie knew they had heard about the Devin girl.

"He knows," Trevor said. "He knows, and he's such a wimp he's crying like a baby." He lowered his foot and kicked the boat. "Probably already told on us, too," he said. "That's the kind of wimp he is."

"I didn't tell," Eddie said. The pain in his hand was intense. He dropped the razor on the seat and rubbed his nose with the back of his right hand. With his other hand, the one he'd cut, he gripped the seat until his knuckles felt as if they would burst apart.

"What are you doing? Praying?" Trevor said. He turned to his brother. "He's turning into his psychoreligious kook of a mother," he said. "He's praying for the salvation of his soul."

"Probably praying we'll go straight to hell, too," Robbie said. "And we should," he added, sniffling.

His brother punched him in the gut. Robbie doubled over and fell onto the sand, whimpering.

"Cut the shit," his brother said. He looked back at Eddie. "How'd you find out?"

"Mrs. Bowen," Eddie said. He held his cut hand against his right side now, and was putting pressure on it by squeezing it between his upper arm and body. He rocked back and forth as he squeezed, fighting the pain. It was bleeding a lot. He could tell by the stain that had spread across the seat and by the way his T-shirt felt damp and sticky where he pressed his hand against it.

"What are you going to do about it?" Trevor said.

"Nothing," Eddie said, gritting his teeth with the pain.

Trevor looked at Eddie for a long time. Eddie looked back, but the boy's face and body were indistinct, blurry, because of the tears in Eddie's eyes. Trevor pointed to Eddie's right side. "What are you hiding?" he said.

"Nothing," Eddie said, looking down.

Trevor stepped into the boat and grabbed Eddie's shoulder. "I said what are you hiding?"

Eddie stopped rocking and looked up at him again. Then he held out his hand. He felt a rush of pain that made him catch his breath when he did.

"Christ," Trevor said, looking at the bloodied hand in the moonlight. Eddie looked, too. The skin he'd cut hung unevenly from two of his fingers. The second web was bleeding, but he hadn't been able to cut through it. The sight of his hand made him dizzy, and he sat back on his feet.

"What the hell did you do?" Trevor asked.

"I'm fixing it," Eddie said.

"Fixing what?" Robbie had recovered, and now stood at the side of the boat, looking down at Eddie.

"My hand," Eddie said. "So it looks like the other one."

"You're crazy," Robbie said.

Trevor just stood there, swaying slightly, and Eddie realized he'd been drinking. "You didn't finish," Trevor said after a while.

"No," Eddie said.

"We'll help," he said. He thought for a moment, then turned to his brother. "Take off your shirt," he said.

"Huh?" the boy said.

"I saw this in a movie. Trust me."

Robbie pulled his T-shirt over his head. His brother took it and tore off a sleeve. He handed the sleeve to Eddie.

"Hold this," he said.

Eddie took the shirtsleeve. His feet had gone to sleep beneath the weight of his body, but he didn't have the energy to move.

"What did you cut it with?" Trevor said.

Eddie picked the razor blade up off the seat. Trevor took it from him and pulled a pint of whiskey out of his back pocket. "I saw this in the movie, too," he said. "We gotta sterilize it so you don't catch gangrene or something." He opened the bottle and poured some of the whiskey on the blade. Then he took a swig for himself.

"Put the cloth in your mouth," he said.

"Why?" Eddie said. He felt as if he were watching this scene from a distance, not participating in it.

"It's to keep you from making too much noise," Trevor said. "Really, I saw it in a movie. We don't want anyone coming down here now, do we?"

Eddie shook his head and did as he was told. The shirtsleeve tasted salty, and reminded him of how thirsty he'd become.

The older boy handed the razor blade to his brother. "Cut it," he said, pointing to Eddie's hand, which now rested on the seat of the boat.

Robbie didn't move.

His brother grabbed him by the hair and pulled so that he was leaning over Eddie. "Cut it," he repeated.

"I can't," Robbie whined. His brother tightened his hold on his hair. "I can't," he repeated.

Trevor grabbed the blade out of his brother's hand and pushed him to the ground.

"I can't believe what I have to put up with," he said. He knelt on the other side of the seat, facing Eddie. "Can you believe what I have to put up with?"

Eddie shook his head, scared by the look on the boy's face, by the thickness of his voice. He knew he should leave, but he couldn't move. Trevor grabbed his wrist and held Eddie's hand down on the seat between them. He held the razor blade in his other hand above the remaining web of skin. "So you didn't tell," he said, tightening his grip on Eddie's wrist.

Eddie shook his head. The taste of the shirt in his mouth sickened him.

"Plan to?" Trevor said.

Eddie didn't answer.

"Well, let's get on with this," Trevor said. "First we should sterilize the area, don't you think? We don't want any infection, do we?" He put the razor on the seat and took the whiskey from where he'd placed it on the floor of the boat. He unscrewed the cap with his mouth and poured some onto Eddie's hand.

Eddie let out a muffled scream.

"See?" Trevor said, spitting the bottle top onto the floor of the boat and turning to his brother. "Now who'd hear *that?*" He turned back to Eddie. "You won't tell, will you?" he said.

Eddie's eyes had filled with tears again and he could no longer breathe through his nose. He tried to spit out the cloth, but Trevor held it in. Eddie pulled his hand from Trevor's grasp and pulled the shirtsleeve out of his mouth. Then he fell to the floor of the boat. He put his injured hand between his legs and squeezed, trying to stop the pain.

"Christ," Trevor said. "A couple of wimps."

Eddie looked at the boy who stood unsteadily above him. In a minute, he thought, I'll stand up to him. When the pain stops, I'll show him.

The sound of cicadas rose from the woods nearby in a long, slow pulse like the beat of a heart. Eddie concentrated on that, trying to forget the pain. He imagined their pulsing sound was Anita Blake's heart beating close to his ear. There was something comforting about its ceaselessness. The sound got louder the more closely he listened. Then he lost it. Maybe a car had passed and quieted them. Maybe a dog or a raccoon.

As Eddie lay there waiting for the sound to return, he remembered that the cicadas were eating the leaves off the trees. They were eating the grass. He realized that if they weren't stopped soon, they would eat everything green.

He heard Robbie speak. "You killed him," he said. He heard the thump of Trevor's fist in his brother's stomach. He heard a groan as Robbie fell once more to the ground.

8. Currents

All through dinner that night, my mother and father and I heard sirens out on the Neck. It wasn't an unusual sound in the summer. The Neck was loaded with what we called summer people, who appeared to have a great deal of money but very little common sense. Over the years, there had been boating accidents and swimming mishaps, but more often than not, according to my father, it was some stockbroker with a fishhook stuck in his index finger.

After dinner, my mother and I sat on the front steps, where she and my father liked to have their after-dinner coffee on summer evenings. From the front steps, they could watch the rest of the world go by. They knew that Mrs. Carr, who worked in Nassau County, usually drove by around seven-thirty and that Mr. Carr, who worked in Manhattan, usually drove by around eight. They could see who took walks together in the evening, who rode bicycles, who jogged after work. They knew that Mr. Cooper had taken up running after his triple bypass surgery, while Mr. Smith, who had also had a heart attack, preferred to take a "brisk constitutional" a few times a week.

Mrs. Bowen pulled into our driveway just after my father had dried the last dinner dish and had come out on the porch to join us. She opened the door and started to get out of her car without unfastening her seat belt. She struggled for a few seconds, then extracted herself from the seat. She stood by the car in her orange house dress, waiting for my parents to join her.

"I suppose you've heard about the Devin girl," she said as my mother approached.

"No," my mother said.

My father and I stayed on the porch, but there was never any question of hearing Mrs. Bowen when she had something to say.

"Why, she drowned," Mrs. Bowen said. "Or her mother drowned her by ignoring her," she said. "Same difference."

I pictured the Devin girl, whom I knew only by sight. She was four or five years old, with a headful of dark curls and huge gray eyes. Her mother, an artist of some kind, was raising her alone. Because her mother was single, she was an outcast in our small community. One could excuse a man like Mr. Carey for not having a wife. One could even feel sorry for him. But there was no excuse for a single mother.

"Oh, my," my mother said. I couldn't see her face, but I didn't need to. She leaned on the hood of the car for support. "What happened?" she said.

Mrs. Bowen raised her voice. "Oh, it's too terrible," she said. "I hate to talk about it. Hate to even think about it." She looked toward the house to make sure I was listening, as if there were some lesson in this story for me. She went on to relate the circumstances of the drowning, editorializing as she did, placing all the blame on Mrs. Devin who, she insisted, everyone had always known was unfit to raise a child.

"Well, you can't blame—" my mother started to say.

"Blue in the face, is what I heard," Mrs. Bowen interrupted. "I hate to even think about it." She opened her car door and got back in. She turned the key in the ignition, and the car made a grinding sound. "Well, look at me," she said, "and just out for a trip to the Dairy Barn before Mr. Bowen gets home." Then she backed out of the driveway, cutting through my father's flower garden, and headed toward town.

No one spoke for a long time after Mrs. Bowen left. I watched my mother. Her hands were out in front of her, and she seemed to be leaning on an imaginary car for support. My father stood beside me on the steps. He had the dish towel flung over his shoulder and looked, quite suddenly, completely worn out.

By the time my mother finally turned around, she'd plastered an everything's okay look on her face. I knew she did this to protect me, and it was one of the things she did that had always aggravated me. It was so dishonest. This summer, there wasn't one thing I could think of that was okay.

"Well," she said, rubbing her hands together as if to get on to the next task. Then she went up the steps and disappeared into the house. My father and I followed, only to find that my mother had gone into their bedroom and shut the door behind her. We stood just outside, hardly breathing, and listened as she dialed the phone.

"Mrs. Devin," we heard her say. "This is Jean Bartlett. You don't know me, I'm a neighbor, but I just wanted to let you know how very sorry I am, and if there's anything I can ever do to—" She stopped speaking suddenly, and in a few moments, we heard her place the receiver back in its cradle. My father left my side and went through the guest bedroom to the back porch, which overlooked the bay—the same bay the Devin girl had drowned in. I followed, and joined him where he sat on the porch swing. The sun had set blood-red over the bay, and we watched the sky as darkness fell.

The tide was on its way out, and as the time passed and the water receded, the smell of the bay turned sour. This had never bothered me before—after all, I'd grown up with it—but tonight its sharp scent of dead shellfish and rotting vegetation was a reminder that everything was either dead or dying, that we were all either dead or dying. I wondered if my father noticed it, too. He put his arm around my shoulder and pulled me close, as if to protect me from an imaginary chill. Then he got the porch swing going, back and forth, back and forth, and rocked me as my mother said he rocked me when I was a baby. The swing creaked in the still, hot night, a counterpoint to the hum of the cicadas in the woods across the inlet. Soon the smell of the bay seemed less offensive, more like what I'd always known.

The house was dark behind us. Though the sun had set, my mother hadn't turned on a single light. She hadn't even left her room, and I pictured her sitting on the bed, staring at the phone, wondering why a woman who didn't even know her wouldn't give her a chance to do what she did best—make everything all right again.

I awoke to the murmur of my parents' voices. My mother had joined us on the porch swing, and I sat between them. My father's arm was still behind me, but now his hand rested on my mother's shoulder.

"She's a good woman," my mother said. "She doesn't deserve this."

"We rarely deserve what we get," my father said gently.

He kissed me on the head. Then my mother kissed me and put her arm behind me, resting her hand on my father's shoulder. The moon rose behind us and lit up the bay. The tide continued to recede. Soon there was hardly any water at all, just rivulets running between large areas of mud. The currents that pulled the water in and out of the bay, the currents that were daily driven by the moon and its phases, flowed far away. But I felt a different current, a much stronger current, running through me, from my father to my mother and back again.

I closed my eyes and let it carry me away.

9. Drifting

A throbbing pain in his hand and the slapping of waves at the sides of the boat were the first things Eddie noticed. He sat up slowly and looked around him. The Careys must have pushed the boat out, but this didn't scare him. He was almost glad of it. It somehow settled things, because although there had been other acts, other insults in the course of their friendship that had been quickly forgotten, he knew he could never forgive them for this.

Eddie had no idea what time it was or how long he'd been drifting, but the boat hadn't gone very far. Sure, he was too far out to swim, but if the Careys had really wanted to get rid of him, they could have tried a little harder. He looked toward shore. Many of the houses were dark and he couldn't see anyone on the beach, but the moon shone a path across the water. He tried to think of what he should do next, but all he could think about was tomorrow, because tomorrow, this day would be only a memory. Tomorrow, finally, he'd change.

There were no oars in the boat, and the clamming rake was gone. The Careys had even taken the broken-down motor. He moved to the front seat and picked up the anchor. He threw it toward shore as far as he could, and then using the thumb and forefinger of his injured hand as a guide, he pulled the boat toward the anchor with his right hand. He felt the cuts open up as he worked, but he kept pulling. When the boat came to a stop, he pulled the anchor slowly from the water and threw it once again toward shore.

Eddie could hear Anita Blake's heartbeat very clearly now. His head rested on her chest, and if he concentrated hard, he could transform the sharp pain in his hand to a dull throbbing that pulsed with the beat of her heart. Anita's body was warm, and he pressed against it in spite of the heavy heat. He wasn't sure how he'd gotten here—his head on Anita's chest, the Carey brothers and everyone else in his life far away. He remembered waking up in the boat and pulling himself to shore. He remembered stumbling on the sand above the high-tide mark. He didn't remember anything after that.

Somewhere in the distance, he thought he heard his mother crying. Somewhere in the distance, he thought he heard his father trying to soothe her. But that was all in the distance. What was close and reassuring and constant was the pounding of Anita's heart.

And then Eddie found himself in his parents' car, sitting between them. His mother had her arm around him and had pulled his head to her chest. Her body was hot, stifling, and he pulled away.

The emergency room doctor told Eddie's parents it was nothing serious. "I'll give him a tetanus booster and get it sewn up in no time," he said.

Eddie's mother looked up. "You can fix it?" she said. Something in her tone alarmed Eddie, and he wriggled uncomfortably on the table, crinkling the paper beneath him in an attempt to get the doctor's attention.

"Sure," the doctor said. "We'll just cut away the extra tissue and stitch it up."

"You can make it the way it was before?"

The doctor looked puzzled. "What?" he said.

"His hand," Eddie's mother said. "You can sew it back the way it was."

Eddie held his breath as he waited for the doctor to respond. He remembered all the times when he was a child and his mother had sat him in her lap and held his hand in hers, examining it like something she'd never seen before, like something Eddie and his father had discovered on the beach and then brought home to show her. She'd sit like that for a long time, mouthing the words to some silent, secret prayer. Eddie could never hear what she was saying, but the air that came from her lips rustled his red hair and tickled his scalp until he couldn't sit still anymore and had to wriggle out of her lap to escape it.

"Excuse me, ma'am," the doctor said, "but that would be ludicrous."

Eddie found he could breathe again. He watched as his mother walked toward the doctor. She stopped when they were face-to-face. "I want my son's hand the way it was before," she said.

Eddie's father held her arm. "Honey," he said. "Let the doctor do what he thinks is best."

She pulled away. "Fix my son's hand the way it was," she repeated.

The doctor looked shocked. "I can't," he said. "I wouldn't if I could, but anyway, there's too much damage."

Eddie watched his mother's expression change. Then she put her hand to her mouth and sank to her knees. "No," she sobbed. "No." Mr. Barnicle leaned over her, and then all Eddie could see was his father's back.

10. Dancing

The day after Nita's mother died, the weather changed. There was a strong wind, and though it was still August and for days before the heat had been intense, I could already feel fall in the air. The damp breeze was chilling, and the sea had begun to churn, raising from the dead the debris on its bottom and releasing a scent that stung my nostrils and made my eyes tear. And of course my eyes were tearing for other reasons, too. First there was Mrs. Bowen's news about the Devin child. The fact that a five-year-old could drown in her own backyard seemed especially cruel to me. And then the very next day we had heard about Mrs. Blake. I couldn't believe I'd never see her again. I found it easier to believe that I'd never see Nita, who had walked away like a stranger the last time I saw her. Still, I had come to the beach hoping to meet her, hoping she'd try to escape her aunts, who were sure to be there for a while, and the beach was our usual refuge.

I sat just above the high-tide mark, which on this day, because of the wind and the waves, was a wide band of seaweed, dead eelgrass, and mussel shells. I wore an old sweatshirt of my father's, and a pair of jeans. I was still having my period, and I felt miserable. The sanitary napkin I wore felt huge but unreliable, and the safety pins I used to keep it in place were poking into my flesh. I hugged the sweatshirt to my chest and buried my bare feet in the sand to keep them warm. The wind was strong, blowing straight onshore, and the waves broke heavily against the shoreline. Though the tide was out and I sat far from the water's edge, I was soon covered by a salty mist. I kept looking beyond the jetty toward Nita's beach, but all I could see was a man being led along the shore by a large black dog.

There was a clatter of wood behind me, and when I turned I saw Nita. She'd dropped the centerboard and rudder on the sand and was heading back across the street for the sail.

"I'm going out," she said from the path. "To hell with you if you won't come."

I scrambled to my feet and ran over the dunes to the road. By the time I got there, Nita had the sail over her shoulder. She crossed the street and passed me on the narrow path, pushing me into the beach grass as she did. I followed her down the path and onto the sand. The sail was balanced awkwardly on one shoulder, and she had to shift her weight back and forth to keep from falling. She walked as if she'd lost her land legs.

We both reached the sailboat at the same time. I hadn't paid much attention to the boat since the last time I was out with Nita, and I was surprised at how worn it looked. We'd turned it upside down after the last time out because there seemed to be a leak where the mast went, and we wanted to drain it. The bottom was a mess. Most of the fiberglass we'd laid over the old wood had worn away, and if I hadn't known it was once painted blue, I'd never be able to tell now. Nita looked from the boat to me when she got to it, but she didn't say anything.

"I'm sorry," I said. My voice came out thin and wavery.

"Well, we knew it was coming, didn't we?" Nita dropped the sail on the ground and flipped the boat.

"They think I'm in my room," she said. She kept her head down as she spoke, and I was glad not to have to look her in the eye. "They hardly came by at all when she was sick, as if she were contagious or something, but now they're here for—at least as long as it takes them to go through everything she owns," she said. "And my father just sits there and takes it."

I remembered meeting her three aunts many summers before. They were all married, but they never brought their husbands when they came to visit the Blakes. The reasons for this had never been explained to me, but I had the feeling that they somehow disapproved of the family.

Nita started tugging on the boat.

"Do you think it's safe?" I said. I'd heard on the radio that morning that there was a small craft advisory, and the only boat I'd seen as I sat looking at the water was the Coast Guard boat, bouncing among the waves and whitecaps like a Ping-Pong ball on a current of air.

Nita glared at me. "Let's not talk, okay?" she said. "If you don't like it, don't come."

I helped Nita drag the boat to the water in silence. We left it half in the water, half out, and went back up the beach and got the sail, centerboard, and rudder. When we started toward the boat again, it was being battered against the sand by the waves. If it had been any weaker, it would have splintered from their force.

When I attached the rudder, I noticed how corroded the pin

was that held it to the boat. The salt had eaten away at it, and I had to hammer it with a rock to loosen it and then attach it. The waves hit me hard as I worked on it, and more than once I nearly lost my balance, but we were soon ready to start out. Because it was so rough, I had to swim the boat out beyond the breaking waves, and when I pulled myself onboard, my jeans and sweatshirt were heavy with water. It had been a while since we'd sailed to-gether—since we'd even talked to each other—and the boat seemed smaller than ever. I sat at the back, working the rudder, and Nita sat in the center holding the sail, but if one of us adjusted her weight even slightly, our legs rubbed against each other or our elbows touched.

Because the wind was blowing straight onshore, it was diffi-cult to get out. Even beyond the breakers, the waves kept trying to send us in, threatening to tip the boat before we had even cleared their crests. After a while, though, we were out far enough to avoid smashing the boat and ourselves on the shoreline. We had to tack to get beyond the Big Rock, and Nita worked the sail silently. The wind was so strong, she had to wrap the rope tightly around her hand to hold on to it, and her fingers were red, puffy with trapped blood. I asked if she wanted to steer, if she wanted me to take the sail, but she didn't answer. She looked straight ahead at the sail, or perhaps right through it. When we were well beyond the Big Rock and the houses on shore looked like Lego toys, I started to worry about how far out we were. Still, I looked ahead and steered the boat in silence. Maybe she couldn't have heard me over the roar of the wind and the sound of the waves, anyway.

When the humidity is low on summer days, it's easy to see Connecticut, a low coastline dotted with cities, sandy cliffs, and smokestacks, but on this day a bank of clouds blocked the view. As I looked over the Sound, I had no trouble understanding how people once thought the world was flat, with defined ends you might disappear over, fall off of, if you went too far. That's how the horizon looked on this day. Like the end of something.

"I think we should tack," I yelled finally.

Nita shrugged, and I took her indifference as a sign that we could. I pushed the rudder so that we turned into the wind. I had to push hard to make it go, because we were going fast and the force of the rushing water was so strong. The turn was rough, and before we got all the way around, two waves washed over the boat. Nita held the sail in, and we both ducked as the boom whipped across. Then she unwrapped the rope quickly from her hand, letting the sail way out as I continued turning.

When we straightened out—I'm not sure now I can describe the feeling I had then. We sailed downwind—the wind at our backs—and it was incredible. We still moved quickly, but it was as if the wind had suddenly died and we were being pushed by the waves, or by necessity and nothing else. They carried us high on their crests and then eased us into the valleys between them like a gentle roller coaster. It was quieter, too. The wind, which had whipped our hair into our eyes and whistled in our ears, now nudged us steadily along, and the only sound was the water rushing alongside the boat. Nita felt this magic, too. Something in her face changed, relaxed, and for a moment she even smiled.

We rode the waves and the wind nearly all the way to the Big Rock before Nita finally spoke. "Let's do it again," she said. "Let's do it one more time." Nita and I worked together then, me turning the rudder slowly as she pulled in the heavy sail, then pushing it quickly for the final part of the turn when she had the sail all the way in. The rudder popped up briefly, and I was afraid we'd miss the turn, but I managed to force it back down. We ducked and slid to the other side of the boat without missing a beat, and we were soon on our way out again, battling the waves, surprised now at the force of the wind in our faces because we'd nearly forgotten it as we sailed with our backs to it.

"This is great," Nita said, wrapping the rope tightly around her fingers again. "This is incredible." She rode that feeling for a while as we rode against the waves, toying with the sail as she'd done earlier in the summer, getting the boat up on its edge until we both screamed and had to lean backward to keep from tipping. Then she seemed to catch herself, feel herself in time once again, because she let the boat down and stopped smiling and stared grimly ahead at the horizon—the place where Connecticut would have been if the world had not so suddenly become flat.

But it *was* incredible.

We went out even farther the second time. We didn't consult each other about when to turn in. I think we both knew how disappointed we'd be when the ride was finally over, when the business of taking down the sail and pulling the boat up the beach would take its place. When we finally did tack, all it took was a meeting of the eyes. No one said "Go." No one said "Duck." We just turned the boat as if it were second nature, as if we'd been sailing under these conditions all our lives.

This time was even better than the first. The momentum of each wave built and built, only to let us down briefly before we were caught up in the next. Maybe the wind had picked up, because the waves seemed higher, and when they lifted us, I felt it in my stomach, a rising excitement.

There were still no other boats on the water. The Coast Guard boat I had seen earlier was nowhere in sight. No one else was crazy enough to be out on a day like this. The sailor was probably in an office at the lighthouse, drinking coffee with his buddies, and awaiting a call of "May Day, May Day" on the radio. But of course we didn't have a radio, and I wouldn't have known enough to call "May Day" even if we had.

A small sailboat heading downwind is even less stable than a small sailboat heading upwind. The slightest shift of weight threatens to upset it, especially when, like our boat, it's filled with water. Then the slightest tilt one way sends all the water in the boat to that side, and you have to use your body to counterbalance all that weight. We did this almost unconsciously, I realize now. Our swaying was just another part of the pleasure of the ride. It was a strange dance we were performing—a dance with disaster, because at any moment the water in the boat could have outweighed us and sent us tumbling into the stormy Sound.

But it didn't happen that way.

What happened was that Nita suddenly let go of the rope and we dove down from the wave we were riding and crashed into the next as if it were a steep embankment. The wave we hit washed over the boat, and then so did another. When the third wave washed over us, Nita went with it. She bobbed up and down next to the boat for a few seconds, laughing and swallowing water, and then she sank. Just like that. I slid into the water where she went under. I wasn't thinking. My clothes were heavy, and I couldn't have pulled her up if I had found her, but there I was, thrashing in the water and screaming her name.

When I began to swallow water, I was scared for myself and swam frantically back to the boat. I dragged myself onboard. I didn't look around me. I didn't for a moment consider going back to shore. I lay there collapsed on the deck, my legs dangling in the water. The waves rocked the boat back and forth, and I might have been seasick if I had been able to feel anything at all. I was too stunned to cry, too stunned to do anything. The chipped paint of the boat was rough against my face. I lay there, devastated, and then I heard Nita's voice.

"You gave up already?" she said. "Is that how much you care?"

I pulled myself up and looked over the other side of the boat. She was resting one hand on the railing. Her head was tilted back, so that only her face was above the water. Her body was under the boat. Her face bobbed up and down on the waves like a buoy, occasionally sinking beneath one when it was too high. She was breathing heavily, and her eyes were very red. She might have been crying.

"Well, don't just sit there," she said angrily. "Help me up."

I helped balance the boat as she pulled herself onboard. When she was seated on the boat, she started to rub her arms, as if to smooth away the goose bumps. I had started to shiver, maybe from the cold, or maybe from the shock of seeing Nita alongside the boat when I thought she had drowned. I wondered how long she had been there, watching me, trying to read my feelings. It must have been a while, I thought. No one can stay underwater that long.

"I thought you had drowned," I said.

"That's stupid," she said. She stopped rubbing her arms and started to scratch them with her long nails. There seemed to be welts all over them. They covered both her arms and were beginning to show on her neck and face.

I looked at the water. The wind and waves had churned up the Sound, and on its surface floated seaweed that usually clung to the rocks on the bottom: alaria, rockweed, mermaid's hair. Then I noticed something else: lion jellyfish. They were red and had long stinging tentacles. There were dozens of them floating between clumps of seaweed. My legs began to itch when I saw them, a sensation that spread over my body like a brush fire the more I counted.

"Do you see them?" I said to Nita.

She kept scratching her arms, staring at something on the deck of the boat that I couldn't see. "I was out here swimming with my mother two days ago," she said. She looked up at me. There was a welt just below her eyebrow, and it had begun to swell so that her eyelid was nearly closed. She looked as if someone had beaten her badly.

"It wore her out," she said. "Do you think that's why she died?"

"No," I said.

"What do you know, anyway?" she said.

I let this pass. "We should go in," I said. "Don't you think?"

Nita shrugged. "What's there to go in for?" she said. "Just some stupid, sniveling relatives who couldn't care less."

"Won't they miss you?" I said. "Won't your father and Denny start looking for you?"

Nita laughed. "Denny? He won't miss me," she said. "He's under his car right now, taking it apart. He's been there since this morning. He got up before the rest of us and just started taking things apart. By the time I got up, both the doors were off. The seats were sitting in the yard. And now he's under the engine. Parts of it are already in a pile in the driveway." She raised both hands to her face and rubbed it brusquely. "I don't know what he's thinking." She rubbed her eyes, then looked at me. "I think he's lost it." She looked down at the deck again.

The waves had turned the boat so that they hit it sideways now. We were rocking violently, and the boom flipped back and forth, out of control. I kept my hand up to catch it on each return, so that neither of us was hit in the head. The boom made a hollow sound each time it hit my hand.

· · ·

We couldn't stay out there forever. We both knew that. My arm soon got tired from catching the boom, so I switched arms. Then my other arm got tired. Nita stopped staring at the deck and started looking around her. We weren't going in or out. Although the waves lifted us and then dropped us back into the valleys between them, we seemed always to be the same distance from shore.

"What do we do now?" Nita said suddenly. I looked at her, surprised, and she started to cry. I put my arm around her, and this time she leaned into me. She put her arms around my neck, her face on my shoulder. "What do we do now?"

I held her. I rocked to the rhythm of the boat. I cried with her. And then I told her to hang on to the rope while I turned the rudder and steered us in to shore.

11. Surfacing

Nita wore a sleeveless black linen dress to the funeral, a dress her mother had bought years before, and one of the few things her aunts hadn't devoured when they descended on the house. Nita wore the dress because it smelled of her mother. It was something she could hold between her thumb and forefinger and feel. Nothing else seemed real—not her father's smile, not Denny's trance-like state as he accepted the condolences of friends and neighbors at the back of the church. And certainly not, for godsakes, Mrs. Bowen's incessant sniffling, which was so loud it traveled to the front of the church, bounced off the altar, and arrived back in the foyer both blessed and amplified.

All through the afternoon and early evening Nita sat in the living room, waving away food as it was offered to her by neighbors, nodding at Molly's mother's repeated assurances that she was always welcome at their house. Her attention kept returning to the coffee table where she had picked up the pair of clamshells for her mother. She could still see their memory etched in the dust of the table like shadows.

When the neighbors had left and her father and aunts had retired to the bedrooms upstairs to grieve and to plunder, Nita left the house and headed across the street to the beach. It was a still night. She avoided the car parts in the yard but nearly tripped over Denny where he lay under what was left of the Dart. He didn't move when her foot hit his, didn't give any indication that he felt anything at all. She only knew he was alive because she saw the beam of his flashlight shift its angle slightly. He hadn't talked to her since the night she had taken her mother to the beach.

Eddie crouched in the crevice between the white rock and the black one. It was midtide, and there was a puddle of water between them, which rose and fell with the waves. The water licked at his calves, and when a big wave hit, it dampened the bottom of his shorts. His legs were beginning to cramp, but he was afraid to move for fear of being discovered by Anita, who sat on a rock a few feet away from him. He'd been watching her a long time, and given the chance, he could watch her forever. She had her back to him, but her silhouette against the moonlight was enough to send a chill down his spine. She was beautiful, mysterious. And she was drawn to the beach the same way he was. Why else would she swim alone in the early morning, or sit alone on the jetty at night? Like Eddie, she found something here that she couldn't find anyplace else.

He imagined what would happen if Anita ever realized how much they had in common. After all, he had lost his mother, too, in a way, the night he had cut away the flesh between his fingers. Maybe some day soon he would sit on the jetty beside her, and she would let him explain.

He heard footsteps approaching from down the beach. Soon Molly stood on the sand looking up at Anita. Anita didn't turn, didn't let on that she knew Molly had arrived, but Eddie saw her shoulders relax in a way that told him she knew Molly was there.

Molly climbed onto the rock next to Anita, and for a while, the two girls sat without speaking. It wasn't an uncomfortable silence, though—the kind Eddie would have with Anita. It was the kind of silence that can happen only between good friends. For days he had wanted to talk to Anita, but now he envied Molly all the things she could leave unspoken as she sat on the rock beside her.

I didn't expect to find Nita on the beach that night. After our last sail, when she had returned home with welts all over her body and had to go to her mother's funeral looking abused and beaten, I was sure her father and aunts wouldn't let her out of their sight again. But there she was, sitting on the jetty, staring at the water.

I climbed onto the jetty and sat on the boulder next to her. She was still wearing the black dress she'd worn to the funeral. It had no sleeves and it hugged her body, emphasizing its curves and making her look older than she was, as if her mother's death had brought her that much closer to her own. We sat for a while without speaking, and then Nita told me—speaking very slowly, weighing her words—that Trevor Carey had called that morning and told her Eddie Barnicle had tried to kill himself.

"He said he did it because of me," she said. "Do you think that's true?" She looked at me.

I shook my head. "Why would anyone do that?" I said.

"What do you know, anyway?" Nita said.

She looked out over the water and then stood up. She put her hands behind her head and unzipped her dress, then pulled her arms through the sleeve holes and wriggled her body so that the dress dropped to the boulder. She was wearing a full slip, and that, too, clung to her. She raised her arms above her head and dove into the dark water.

I jumped off the jetty onto the sand and watched her.

I soon realized that Eddie Barnicle stood beside me. I hadn't even heard him approach. One of his hands was wrapped in gauze and hung lamely at his side. He was so close that if I moved even slightly, I would brush against the bandage. I stood still, scanning the water for signs of Nita. She surfaced a few times but always went under again.

When Nita reached the Big Rock she lifted herself gracefully onto its seaweed-covered crown, which was just beneath the surface. She looked as if she were crouching on the water. Eddie breathed a series of long, anguished sighs beside me. When Nita rose to her feet, her slip an eerie glow in the moonlight, he held his breath.

Nita raised her arms and turned slowly around, a queen acknowledging the cheers of her people, a priestess worshipping the goddess of the moon. Eddie raised his injured hand, as if he could reach out and pull her to shore. The gauze bandage glowed like Nita's white slip.

I didn't know whether the tide was coming in or going out. When the moon is full, the tide rises and falls quickly. I didn't know whether Nita would rise above the water as the tide receded, like a saint ascending, or whether the water would rise and cover her, return her to the sea.

I reached for Eddie's hand and pulled it down, held it still.

"Did you do it for her?" I said.

Eddie looked at his bandaged hand. Then he looked at Nita, standing on the Big Rock, staring up at the moon. "No," he said finally. "Not really."

I stood silent, wanting him to say more. He examined the bandage in the moonlight while I waited. "I did it for me," he said.

I thought about this. Then I took off my shorts and T-shirt and dove into the water.

That night, there were no jellyfish. That night, the water didn't glow as it parted and then closed behind me. It was cool, dark, and thrilling. It tightened my skin, made me feel as if I had finally grown to fit it. I wasn't afraid. I thought only about reaching Nita. The moonlight made a path across the water, and I believed that she knew where it led.

When I reached the Big Rock I tried to pull myself up. Its surface was slippery, covered with mermaid's hair, and I slid back into the water many times before I was able to stand beside Nita. I looked for Eddie Barnicle on the shore. He was nowhere in sight, but in a moment, I saw his head bob to the surface, halfway between the beach and the Big Rock. He was on his way out to join us.

"I thought you might stay out here and be covered by the sea," I said to Nita.

"Did you come out here to rescue me?" she said.

I nodded.

Nita was silent for a long time. "You don't know anything," she said at last. "You never did." I was ready to slide back into the Sound and leave her forever when I saw her smile.

Jane Hosie-Bounar grew up on Long Island, where *Life Belts*, her first novel, takes place. She graduated from Middlebury College, received an M.A. in creative writing from Syracuse University, and has worked as a free-lance writer and editor and as a fiction workshop instructor.

She and her husband Khaled Hosie Bounar live in Concord, Massachusetts, with their two daughters.

Life Belts is the winner of the Tenth Annual Delacorte Press Prize for a First Young Adult Novel.